T0033461

TO

THE

FOREST

TO THE FOREST

ANAÏS BARBEAU-LAVALETTE

translated by **RHONDA MULLINS**

COACH HOUSE BOOKS, TORONTO

Coach House Books acknowledges the financial support of the Government of Canada for the translation of this book. We are also grateful for the generous assistance for our publishing program from the Canada Council for the Arts, the Ontario Arts Council, and the Department of Canadian Heritage through the Canada Book Fund.

LIBRARY AND ARCHIVES CANADA CATALOGUING IN PUBLICATION

Title: To the forest / by Anaïs Barbeau-Lavalette ; translated by Rhonda Mullins
Other titles: Femme forêt. English
Names: Barbeau-Lavalette, Anaïs, author. | Mullins, Rhonda, translator.
Description: Translation of: Femme forêt.
Identifiers: Canadiana (print) 2022047737X | Canadiana (ebook) 20220477396 | ISBN 9781552454633 (softcover) | ISBN 9781770567597 (EPUB) | ISBN 9781770567603 (PDF)
Subjects: LCGFT: Novels.
Classification: LCC PS8603.A705 F4413 2023 | DDC C843/.6—dc23

To the Forest is available as an ebook: ISBN 978 1 77056 759 7 (EPUB), ISBN 978 1 77056 760 3 (PDF)

I want to be outdoors, to have no outlines or edges, to not be held back in any way. The ceilings are too low and the walls too close.

I watch all the lives I let go by without me.

They are calling to me, so I open the windows. There is a draft in my house.

I am caught between the inside and the outside world.

On windy days, I wonder whether my roots will hold.

Whether a storm will rip me from the earth where my children learned to walk.

Whether I will be able to stay.

I find a splinter under my skin. The memory of a forest.

You're the one who makes beauty.
– Maman

Do not describe things
as they happened;
make them legends.
– Romain Gary

When they strung the yellow crime-scene tape around the park, I left the city, with my family under my coat.

Relieved I could protect them.

That winter, I move into the Blue House. I am not just passing through. I am not on vacation.

We live here together, two families, in the forest. Four adults and five children, aged three to nine.

My parents settle into the Red House down the road.

The valley will be our refuge for months.

When I get to the end of the frozen road, I hide away, wrapped in my three children.

Their warmth takes a while to calm me.

I am terrified at the immense void ahead of us.

The wind is blowing on the creaking roof. My children are an ephemeral shell that covers my body.

My mind gets lost in the abyss of the forest that swallows us up.

The large birch at the edge of the woods is dying in the cold. It pitches, dry, eviscerated, bare.

I am like the tree. Made of the same atoms of carbon, nitrogen, and oxygen. My genes, structured in a DNA double helix, have the same architecture and workings as its genes.

And I am the fruit of the same event: the appearance of life on Earth, billions of years ago.

It bends. It's going to break.

But underground, its strong, full roots, thirsty and brave, hold it upright.

And it recovers, stretching into the night. Scathed, but standing.

I would like to be a grey birch. I cling to my children.

I dip into a waking slumber. Captive, caught between awake and asleep.

My parents' Red House was built at the edge of a pine forest much older than them.

I am still a little girl when they move in.

I don't know the land will become mine.

But my fingers are already making it mine, scratching at the earth, entrusting it with my dead.

A dozen guinea pigs, my cats, my grandparents are laid there, one by one, filling the field with their recollections, nourishing the clover with their memories.

When I am on the threshold of adolescence, a small tent village is erected crookedly on these memories, the promontory for our electric bodies that boldly go into the night.

It's party time. The fire soaks the skies; our cries as young shoots join those of the coyotes on the other side of the mountain.

My parents pull their car into the tall grass, and the music rings out from the trunk. They savour our gentle, indomitable freedom before going to bed.

That's how they managed to keep me close. They expanded the nest, wove it from wild grass and hay.

They go to bed in the Red House as we go single file, slicing through the field, parting the tide of fireflies as far as the cold stream, which we throw our bodies into.

I am fourteen, and I flit boy to boy, singing 'Alegría.'

This is my mother's land and my heritage.

I have travelled the world, and when I think of home, I think of here.

Of my father making bonfires and bouquets of four-leaf clovers, of my mother crossing the pine forest, determined, as if taking root with each step, a small procession of hens at her heels.

Of my parents' storms that seem bigger here because everything has more room to be, including pain.

Things often blew up, with shouts and tears and me in the middle, loving them both.

Forty-five years interweaving one life with the other, taking back one's own for a while with a piece missing, changing with the other, for the other, because of the other.

They loved other skin, kissed other faces with all the newness that they offered, caught their breath. They sculpted from clay and sleet what was next in their partnership.

His eyes are blue like a cold, cloudless sky on a winter morning.

Her eyes are black like heavy, moist, freshly turned soil.

An endless love that continues to teach me everything I know.

When I was young, they put the hook of life into me, so I could never tear free. So I would be obliged to take it whole. When everything crumbles, a connection holds me to the pulse of the world, and they are the ones who made it for me.

As soon as the first dandelions broke through the concrete on the sidewalk, my mother would gather them, the first of the season. Dandelions heal themselves. When you rip them out, five flowers bloom over the wound. My mother would bring home her bouquet of warriors: flowers from concrete, with petals like the mouth of a beast, *dents de lion* – lion's teeth – that grow despite the cold and the city.

Flowers that fight, flowers of promise, flowers salvaged after the winter.

My mother made life a celebration, come what may.

Whenever an ambulance went by, rather than wishing for the healing of the injured or the reanimation of the lifeless, my mother would light up, saluting 'a woman giving birth' as she passed. Together we would wave into the distance toward the wailing sirens, associated for me with the clamour of good news.

It was by design; it might have been a lie, but it was the way the world was orchestrated, and what I learned above all was that its music belonged to us. That one day it would be my turn to take the baton and choose what could emerge from the chaos.

My father makes dancing birds with dead branches and is fascinated by a researcher who has recorded the sleep waves of a rabbit, awed by the idea that we can 'hear them dream!'

He was a young communist, travelled the world, survived earthquakes and hostage takings. He is the best person to explain to me injustice and its workings. But there is still lightheartedness in his eyes, the suppleness of a detour that ushers me to the other side of it all, just beside what is glaring. My father has a penchant for wonder and finds four-leaf clovers without looking, or, rather, they find him. My father is also a good-luck charm.

When there is no more beauty, it is because of them that a piece of me still clings to the source, the magma, to what doesn't vanish into thin air.

The Blue House is overcrowded.

At first, we are effervescent, tangled together in bubbly happiness. Then we draw lines and glare.

We will have to respect how each person is and lives. We will have to set aside our moods and become impervious to those of the others.

We will need to be supple and humble. And swallow by the shovelful our need for freedom.

And we will need rules. Lots and lots of rules.

I inherited my father's gift: I find clovers like dandelions. I dry them between the pages of the books lying around me, which I promise myself one day I will read.

I have never stooped over for any other plant. They fade into complete anonymity, both too familiar and too foreign.

I cross the pine forest of my childhood. Half my life took shape between these towering trees.

The tips of the pine needles create an invisible rain, a cloud of molecules: negative ions. Science has shown their incredible power. Negative ions make you happy.

A fragile, brittle momentum surges within me. The crumbs of a new desire.

There is nothing abrupt or risky about it. It is not a normal desire.

I want to knit a path between me and the rest of the world.

I spend time with plants without really knowing them; they are in my path and no longer surprise me. A bit like everyday people, the ones we pass so often we forget to see them.

Natural beings must be like cherished beings: if I want to love them all, first I have to love them one by one.

Mary used to live a little way down the dirt road.

Of Ukrainian origin, Mary seems to have emerged from her garden, her pretty, round, white head popping up among the lupins.

She lives stooped over her flowers and her cats.

Her favourite has three legs.

Mary, hunched in love, raised her four children here, with no running water.

The closest spring is far off in the forest; she jerry-rigged a pipe to connect her house to it.

As I walk past her Blue House, hungover in short shorts, holding my best friend's hand, I dream of living here one day, perched over the stream.

In the meantime, we share Mary's warm bread in her wrinkled Blue House, which has been watching over the frogs since 1880.

The neighbour down the road, the filmmaker and passionate sovereigntist Pierre Falardeau, sometimes comes to drink tea with Mary, in the shadow cast by the Canadian flag that floats innocently over the house.

Out here, politics erode, swallowed by the forest.

'I hated his movie *Elvis Gratton*. But I love Pierre. He's a gentleman.'

Mary is my English grandmother. I love to wrap my arms around her and tuck my face in the crook of her rippled neck. I listen to Beck, I wear barrettes and overalls, I drink raspberry coolers in the alleyways, I neck with boys to Led Zeppelin, but already I want to grow old like Mary.

Holding my own against winters in the valley, chopping my own wood, baking bread, and talking to the faithful flowers that return every year. The very first, bright blue and hardy, carpeting the ground under the old tree, before its leaves steal their light. They are Mary's favourite. I don't know yet what they are called.

The old tree in front of the Blue House is named Bertolt. The children baptized him as soon as they could talk. It is one of their first words, a primitive anchor for the house that Mary will leave to us when she goes.

Bertolt is a pirate ship, a fortress, a desert island, a dojo. In addition to a ladder and a swing, along his flanks he has cavities that serve as beds, cradling scraped, brave little bodies.

The children become lords of the canopy. Like our ancestors, they live in the tree, travelling branch to branch. We have kept a thumb in memory of this first habitat, a fifth finger that we still share with monkeys.

The group of children walk along Bertolt's pathways and slip their treasures under his bark, tucked in the grooves made by ants. The mushrooms from the old tree feed their potions. Bertolt keeps secrets and shelters the dead bodies of the little beasts they collect.

Up there, they are as one, and they protect each other from falling. Bertolt's crown must be a place of solidarity, or one of the little warriors could plummet.

Our long-ago life spent in the trees gave us frontal vision, eyes that face forward, allowing us to gauge depth, essential for moving branch to branch.

Unlike animals that have eyes on either side of their faces, our field of vision is more limited. Therefore, the vision of others has long been an extension of our own.

Hence the need to live in groups.

Students of human evolution have determined that we were social animals primarily due to vulnerability. We need others so we don't die.

That spring, we don't know whether the old tree is going to make it. Its long branches groan under the feather weight of its inhabitants.

In ceremonial excitement, we lop off pieces of Bertolt.

Our soaring hope is a barricade against the end of his days.

One of his large limbs is torn off and lies on the ground.

Is Bertolt dead?

Thick knots form in the children's throats.

Time stops; we look for signs of life. We don't want Bertolt to lie down on the little sailors between two storms.

Suddenly, a miracle.

'Maman! Bertolt is bleeding!'

Maple sap drips on his shoulder. We rush to collect the sweet water.

We attach makeshift pots to the ends of the remaining limbs, adding glass jars and anything that can contain the water from the survivor. Bertolt is beautiful. All dressed up, decorated with medals.

The holy water will be boiled and savoured.

The old tree is ready for boarding for another season. His buds sprout quickly, revealing hundreds of little secrets: they tell us that Bertolt is a black maple, that his three-lobed leaves will soon be out.

There are very few black maples left in the country, even in the world.

Bertolt is a rare bird.

At his base, stuck to his hard bark, a smaller tree is growing, fragile and tender and yet soon ready to take up the torch.

It comes from the same seed as Bertolt.

It is called 'gourmand' in French, 'tràgon' in Spanish, 'ghiotonne' in Italian, and 'sucker' in English. It is the sequel to a tree.

Its memory, its immortality.

This moving phenomenon is what makes it such that, today, the oldest tree in the world is 43,000 years old. It is called the *Lomatia tasmanica*. The royal holly of Tasmania. A contemporary of Neanderthal man.

All our efforts, all our tragedies, all our discoveries, all our victories, all our sorrows: the whole history of our species is contained in the one life of the *Lomatia*.

My grandfather Jacques also loved Mary and her Blue House.

Jacques spent his life working the market in Paris. He hawked vegetables on Rue Mouffetard, with his blue apron, his red cheeks, and his cold nose.

'Fresh cauliflower, try the leeks, two francs a bunch! That's right, lady, two francs a bunch.'

I visit him and my grandmother Boubou every summer. I am at the beginning of the world, everything about to unfold before me.

I fly alone with my long bare legs, a new source of power I am learning to wield.

In the little, narrow bathroom that smells of blue urine, I kiss the passenger who has followed me here right on the mouth. He has dreadlocks and olive skin. We share Walkman earphones and caress each other under the paper-thin Air Transat blankets while listening to Metallica's 'Nothing Else Matters.'

Then I take the Paris metro, with my large pack on my back. I get off at the Mairie d'Ivry station, at the outer edges of Paris. I walk up the hill, tired from the trip, but carried along by the grace of vacation. It smells of boxwood and cold sweat: I love it. It's Paris.

At the top of the hill, I cross the cemetery. It is the shortcut to the public housing project where my grandparents live. The one where my father was born and grew up.

From the middle of the cemetery, I see Boubou on her balcony, wearing her red sweatshirt and standing behind her begonias; she may have been waiting there for me since morning. She sees me through her thick glasses. I pick up the pace. I am eager to settle into her sweet fragrance.

The elevator is narrow; its mirrored door from another age takes its time closing. Everyone in the building travels in this tiny space. It smells of sweat, rain, flesh, sorrow, and desire. The tired damp of immigrants, factory workers, and mothers. Sixth floor: I get out.

I approach the door, which is already open, and their warm wind fills the space. Boubou and Jacques, so happy to see me, like a miracle they can't get over.

She thinks I've grown. I wash ashore in her arms, in her powerful smell of burnt caramel that I can find nowhere else and that I will spend my life looking for. The ultimate comfort.

I am lucky to have learned how to hug. To seize the people I love with my whole body. To surrender to the embrace. My arms open to them, I dive into theirs. Even those who are difficult to hold. This contact helps me discover what is under the skin, behind the gaze.

The table is already set, just for me. A big bowl of hot chocolate, baguette, butter, cheese. Boubou will sit down and watch me eat. Jacquot will go for a walk with his music in his ears.

He likes to walk the streets of Paris listening to accordion tunes.

He will come back around noon, bring me Flanby crème caramel, and we will eat tinned green beans and pasta with ketchup while watching *Des chiffres et des lettres*.

Jacquot never talks about the war he fought or the one he fled. The only thing I know is that he went hungry.

When the meal is over, he carefully wipes a bit of bread over each plate. 'Waste not, want not,' he says, more for himself than for us. It is his prayer.

The plates are clean and empty. It's nap time.

Boubou sings 'Salade de fruits, jolie, jolie, jolie' while she folds laundry, and Jacques curls up in their big bed, window open to the sky.

I open a can of maple syrup while my grandmother looks on, contented. In the large wooden pantry set against the wall, forty-two cans of maple syrup sit idle. Boubou asks us for a new one every time we come.

But they don't use it. It's for 'company.' 'Company' is us.

Boubou watches me use an old calculator, astonished; she calls to Jacques so I can show him how gifted I am: 'I mean, have you seen all the things she knows how to do … !' They look at me together, satisfied. 'Our work won't have been for nothing.'

Words I wear as a necklace.

And when Boubou receives the recording of the choir of a hundred children I sing in, she listens to it solemnly. In the choir, in the midst of ninety-nine other children's voices singing 'Silent Night,' she recognizes mine. 'She sings so beautifully … !' That's love.

One morning, I wake up a little early, and I find Boubou in the kitchen, a beer in hand. She sees me see her, and she hides the bottle for the sake of appearances. She can't drink beer in front of her granddaughter at seven in the morning.

Afterward, she is in a bad mood. Jacques opens the balcony door, whistling, his heart light, and exclaims at an insect that flits past him and darts around the tidy little living room: 'Look, Boubou, a pretty butterfly!'

But Boubou doesn't turn her head toward the thing beating its wings in her living room. She says to Jacques, 'Kill it. It will make caterpillars,' folding her dishcloth perfectly.

She shoots me a fierce look. Reminds me that I know nothing of life, of her life.

I know nothing of all the hangers that tore out the beginnings of children clinging in her belly. I know nothing of the great love that got away. I know nothing of the weight of sacrifice and the crumbled dreams.

Jacques looks at me, caught off-guard. Jacques cannot disobey Boubou.

But Jacques doesn't want to kill anymore.

Both of them, suddenly frozen in a corner of their pain, watch the insect flying.

These are the pieces that make real people.

And often the hidden angles are essential to love.

So I do it. I climb on the sofa, I reach my arm up, and I crush the butterfly. It leaves a white stain on the flowered wallpaper. The remains of two little torn wings on the living room wall.

When I go to France, I visit castles, cave paintings, museums, and markets. I pay my respects to Jim Morrison at the Père Lachaise cemetery, and I collect looks from men – not something that happens at home – while having a beer on a terrace. I am free and beautiful wherever I go.

But for me, France, the real France, is found on the sixth floor of the Ivry-sur-Seine public housing project. On the other side of the cemetery, sitting in a Mickey Mouse nightgown, nestled between my grandparents.

Boubou and Jacquot are the most beautiful port of call in the world, the Parisian alcove of my adolescence, where I smoke Amsterdamer rolled cigarettes out the window while looking at the moon, spellbound by the life that lies ahead of me.

One day, Boubou dies. In her casket, I place a bag of soft caramels that I brought her from home. I want my grandmother to be cremated with them. The pinnacle of her perfume. I want a caramelized grandmother.

My mother cries while reading the recipe for yogurt cake that Boubou made so well, while my brother plays 'Ode to Joy' on the trumpet.

I know that my father and my uncle had major discussions about the ashes. That is what it is like to be one of two siblings on either side of the world.

I know that part of my caramelized grandmother is in the valley behind me. She rests alongside Suzanne Meloche, Marcel Barbeau, Pauline Barbeau. And, soon, Jacques Lavalette and Mary Poulos.

After Boubou's death, Jacquot is alone. There are no more big lunches on the kitchen table. There is only one plate to wipe clean and no one left to water the begonias.

Jacquot wants to live in the Red House. He dreamed of Canada as a young man. And now he is an old man, mischief in his eyes, wearing navy Bermudas, whistling down the dirt road toward Mary's house.

'My French is quite ill.' Mary has done her hair. Her piercing blue eyes are twenty years old.

Jacques wants to take English lessons with her. He goes to the Blue House every day. He is a poor student, remembers nothing.

Mary doesn't give up.

'Jacques, repeat after me: I am a man.'

Jacques protests. No, not at all. Mary is not *a man, no no no.* Mary is a woman, oh yes!

Mary hesitates, doesn't know whether to laugh. Her student is a class clown. His little blue eyes are like two surprises, his wide smile reveals his nice white teeth like 'mouse tracks in the snow.'

'Okay, Jacques, let's go for a walk.'

Mary takes my grandfather's hand, and together they cross the little bridge that leads to the field of milkweed. Jacques slows down over the water, and his other hand squeezes Mary's arm. Like a child clinging to his mother.

'Are you all right, Jacques?'

'It's the water. I'm afraid of the water.'

Jacques doesn't know how to swim. We know he almost drowned, but he won't tell us where or how.

Mary holds my grandfather with a firm hand, and together they slice through the fields, splendid as they pass. Combined, they are 160 years old. The sun knows it and shows its reverence.

It is mild and lush, the green is teeming, and the land is settling into the wild, untamed bed of summer.

Jacquot leaves us at the peak of the season. He returns to the window of his public housing unit, in Ivry-sur-Seine.

He won't be back.

One morning, he tunes his little radio to opera.

He drags a chair and leaves it between the bed that is now too big and the window that is now too small for the air he requires.

He folds a delicate cuff at the bottom of his blue canvas pants and slowly buttons his purple cardigan. He looks at himself and thinks he is still handsome. He has had a good life, all things considered.

It is that bit of abyss inside him that sucks him up. The parents that he never had, and that he so needs right now. His entire body tells him that he is old, but he feels like he is still in short pants and can't remember how to tie his shoes.

Boubou's jewellery boxes sit under the mirror. Beads and junk jewellery, a watch stuck on the same second, a ballerina in a tutu who no longer twirls. Jacquot brushes his thick, tired finger over them.

Then an invisible hand helps him climb onto the wobbling chair. Jacques looks into the distance, and the branches of the old sycamore wave in time with his heart.

Down below, five identical balconies in a row. One day, Moumousse, his grey cat, fell six floors and broke his paw.

Jacques sets a foot on the railing, grips the shutters, and places the other foot beside the first. There. Jacques is now precariously balanced, standing on the window frame.

Jacques is not a cat.

Two feet side by side and his entire body suspended between air and ground. Jacques is the floating fluff of a dandelion. The wind blows on him. He takes flight.

My father leaves for France the next day. My brother and I don't know what's going on. My mother is left alone with a tragedy that just loomed in the middle of the road.

She searches for a way to tell us our grandfather has killed himself.

I don't know whether she knows that in my eyes he is the absolute incarnation of happiness. A man who savours everything. His lopsided laugh, his eternal love of women, and the sort of profound kindness that makes true heroes.

My mother takes us to a restaurant. Over a plate of mussels, I learn that my favourite grandfather has killed himself.

I know I screamed. And that I immediately wanted to know how he did it.

Oddly, the answer soothed me. Because I could find the poetry in it. His head didn't explode; he didn't poison himself.

Although I sometimes thought of whoever found him on the ground. Crushed on the pavement.

Since then, when the little umbrella of a dandelion floats through the air, I don't catch it to make a wish, like I did when I was little. Instead, I blow hard on it to keep it aloft, so it never sets down. I take refuge with him on the wind, which carries a light piece of fluff over the streets of Paris. I can even overlay a little accordion music.

I have no scruples about taming violence. I am sovereign. I invent memory as I see fit.

There is a tree that doesn't die. It is called the bristlecone pine, and it doesn't age.

It can be killed, but it is programmed not to die. Ever.

I recently learned that Mary raised from those around her the money needed for her trip. She had planned to leave her Blue House to explore the Quais de la Seine on Jacques's arm.

Jacques is gone, and Mary falls in the snow. She hurts her leg and resigns herself to selling her house.

She walks through the storm to the Red House and tells my father she is leaving. 'And my house is for your daughter.'

Her house is for me.

I am pregnant. I can't leave this house and the memories it has soaked up to anyone else. No way.

I take the hand of the friend with whom I so often walked along the road and who knows what Mary's bread tastes like. Together, with our men, we come ashore on our island.

In the years that follow, I visit Mary in the residence in the village. She is on the first floor of a long brown building that always smells like soup.

I am weighed down with an infant seat in which a pile of flesh has surrendered to sleep and two little whiz kids who use the long, straight hallway and its brown carpet as a racetrack. One by one, the doors creak; old people emerge, dumbstruck by the sudden life in their halls.

We storm Mary's tiny apartment. A small room, which she has turned into a jungle, where her five cats have settled in the climbing plants. Mary has made quilts for each of my children, and today she gives me one for the sleeping baby.

Then she shows me her treasures. Because Mary is a collector, and her foraging keeps her alive. Every day, she goes to Maison Reilly, in the heart of the village. On the first floor, her friends serve a daily special. On the second floor is the twenty-five-cent clothing bazaar. But the basement is where the panacea is found.

Porcelain, wax dolls, old magazines, and vintage posters.

That day, Mary proudly takes out of her closet a huge washed-out photo that is rippled in its frame. She wants to give it to my father.

'I thought he would love it.'

I leave with three superheroes in quilted capes and a gigantic, laminated, washed-out image of the Eiffel Tower, too big for me to close the trunk. It is cold in the car, but I can't refuse Mary anything.

When I travel, I send her postcards. When I go to the village, I visit her. But my visits grow more infrequent, and Mary moves to a long-term-care facility. I don't see her again for far too long.

Only her massive picture is still centre stage in the Blue House. Her little white head pops up from the lupins.

It is this house, filled with her stories, that becomes our shore for the coming months. Mary's photo has yellowed on the wall, the mice rule the roost, and the ants nibble on what is left of the walls.

First, there is euphoria: running toward a horizon that belongs to no one. The pristine valley does not crack under the children's feet; their fury explodes into a thousand cries of joy in the deserted flatlands and echoes off the nameless trees.

The snow blankets the field. I walk through the fragile perfection. I slice through the white, and I search for my words. The magnificent, majestic countryside is all around me and under my feet. The land holds me. But the words I have left for talking about it are dry and empty. Even the word 'nature' disintegrates; it no longer has lustre or light.

We will have to put words back in the world.

It will be a rebirth.

Our weeks are organized into chapters. The adults each lead one afternoon of classes; we do a big grocery shop every two weeks. Sunday is day zero: we cook and tidy anew.

Our routine is like a signpost stuck on the fridge, where the children come to get their bearings several times a day. And in the night, sometimes, the adults do too.

The news tells us it is going to be a while yet.

Bent over a piece of wet bark, my son applies himself to raising the sails. I offer my shoelace as a guyline. It is an outing for just the two of us; we have escaped the rest of the herd. Braving the cold on our bikes to the next bridge, we set off on a voyage along the shore of the stream, and we make boats.

With his fingertips red from the cold, Noé polishes the rudder.

We approach a boat launch. A small act for a long voyage.

The source of the Ruiter Stream is up on the mountain. In the heart of the forest, in the depths of Lake Fullerton. That used to be the starting point for logs sent by the drivers downstream by the hundreds, winding through the country to the United States.

The foghorn sounds. On the beach, Noé is finishing his ark made of bark; he entrusts to it a twig captain, his arms thrown open to the water.

Noé whispers a secret to him (he is the king of secrets) and places the boat in the eddy, which carries it off immediately.

It will follow the Ruiter Stream to the majestic Missisquoi River, then end up in Lake Champlain. From there, its captain will have the choice between New York, via the Hudson, and everything along the St. Lawrence River, via the Richelieu.

We are silent for a moment before the endless possibilities.

This child handles wonder with the delicacy of a sage.

Interested by what emerges from the ground, the sky, and the water, he stoops between two gusts of wind, delicately making a reverent gesture to the living.

We get back on our bikes, hands now petrified in the cold. On the way home, a family of wild turkeys lazily watches us as we pass.

A car slows down. It is my neighbour, Hermann, looking solemn, and his wife, Angélique, at his side.

He lowers the window. The icy wind blows on his face, his eyes look straight into mine. He tells me he is sick, that he is going to die.

He invites me to come over for a coffee. Angélique is crying, and he raises the window.

Noé loses a tooth. It's hard to ride a bike with a baby tooth in your hand. He entrusts it to me. I am so afraid of dropping it, I hold it in my mouth. We're almost home.

The warm house awaits us. Noé tells the story of the expedition while he drinks a hot chocolate.

That evening, on a piece of paper he slips under his pillow, Noé writes in a careful hand: 'Dear Tooth Fairy, I'm not interested in money. Wow me.'

I knew this child would keep throwing me off balance. He was born in a car on the side of the highway. He can't stop there.

In the middle of a traffic jam, I'm breathing. Outside, everything is grey and unmoving. Inside, it's moving.

I am stretched out on the backseat of a rusted old car, inherited from the aunts who rescued and raised my mother. A loving car, beige and clean: the champagne car. My man grips the steering wheel, glaring at the horizon as if to make it come to him.

I can't catch my breath.

'The head is here!'

We're almost there. I know it. But I can't wait. The head is here, on the side of the highway. The champagne car stops on an angle in front of the Couche-Tard. My man leaps out, shouting for help, before leaning over me. Our eyes hold each other so we don't lose control. Death, which doesn't frighten me, suddenly comes to lay its heavy coat over me. Over my child. I start to lose it, the pain shoots up to my head, grips my entire being. I start to slide, not knowing what to grab on to. Outside it is cold and ugly, no refuge. Except him, suddenly larger than life. The man I have so often consoled, his fragility in the palm of my hands, that man becomes a tree. A solid oak on the side of the highway, a break that promises victory in an urban desert.

The 911 operator asks, 'Is the lady breathing?'

The 'lady' in question is me. Whose belly is shape-shifting. My hands tear at the damp car seat, while this oak of a man grounds himself in the parking lot for the delivery. On the highway, the stream of people going somewhere continues.

Help!

The baby wants to come, but I have never been so scared. I'm scared his heart will tire, scared that the cold will snatch him from me, scared my baby will be swallowed up by the grey, by the ugliness.

Darkness. My eyes closed. Cling to them, escape. First to my mother. My volcanic mother my mother who dances my mother love my screaming mother my mother who watches over me and who says: 'You're the one who makes beauty.'

Okay. Okay, Maman.

And cling to the others, all the others.

On the side of the highway, parked on an angle in the Couche-Tard parking lot, I cross the oceans, I stride through the hamlets of summits, I plunge into the hollows of the anthill cities, I scrutinize the deserts of snow and war. And I draw closer to all the women in the world, sweaty and powerful. I join with them, loving. I merge with them, their blood, their spit, their sex. Their hot breath on my neck, the smell of their blood in my mouth, their water on my thighs. I give birth with them.

The child is born in the amniotic sac: he is born en caul. My man catches him in his bubble. A fish in its ocean: his little mouth that opens to the sky, his little body still protected from the world.

With a scraped finger, a broken nail, the hand of a musician, the most beautiful hand in the world, your father tears open your wrapping.

The water drains over him. You are here. Your black eyes utterly surprised. Your little purple body that flashes its newness to the slumbering motorists. They have forgotten the beginning. You are here to remind them.

Your father lays you on top of me. This is where I meet you. My little slippery purple king.

Are you alive?

Emergency services asks, 'Is the child breathing?' You are silent. The teenage cashier from the Couche-Tard flutters around us, bewildered. She is sixteen, with pink hair, having the fright of her life. She is our makeshift nurse. Alarmed, she runs to get a shoelace to tie off the cord, she runs to get a warm blanket, she runs, in shock from the violent breach in her day: a sticky newborn is fading in her parking lot.

My oak of a man reaches through the unknown with broad, gentle, confident gestures. Grounded and fully present.

The child is not crying, the child is purple, but my man reassures the emergency services: 'No, Madame, the cord is not around his neck.'

He pushes away fear with his heartbeat and brings about the birth of our son.

We make a symphony of the concrete, a happy resistance.

Sirens in the distance: the police. The sky clouds over, a looming storm. I hold you to me, and suddenly I feel it. The pliant beat. The beginning of your life. And finally you cry. Our king is called Noé, and he begins his journey in a champagne car on the side of the road.

That day reveals the most majestic of the three of us.

Once the children are asleep, nothing is more important than finding something better than the Tooth Fairy's two dollars. A few of us set to the task and come up with a talisman made from recycled jewellery and bits of the outdoors.

Now we need to slip it under Noé's pillow. Five of us sleep in the same room. If I fail, three little witnesses will awaken. I feel hot.

I have travelled the world, often alone. I have lived in a war zone. I have been threatened with a knife and a Kalashnikov. But nothing has ever frightened me more than this moment on tiptoe when I lift the pillow.

Holding imagination like this, holding in my hands the fleeting connection to the other land, I find myself before the vivid immediacy of the end of childhood and the immensity of that grief.

Noé's closed eyes are like two drawn ink lines, perfect calligraphy. His breath merges with his brother's. My shaking hand places it, there, just a bit of magic. The most important gestures are not always the biggest.

As soon as he could talk, Noé asked for a tree.

He wanted a weeping willow.

We planted it on his third birthday. His grandfather, wielder of shovel; the child, wielder of pride. So little and so naked in front of the frail tree, barely taller than him, his hand slung around it as if around the neck of a new friend.

Today, when the water of the stream rises, it generously laps at the trunk of the weeping willow, which is courageously stretching out above the high waters, like the child.

Francis Hallé resembles a tree. You take on the features of those you spend time with, those you love. His face ripples like the hardened bark of mature trees, his body seems to be planted deep into the earth, immovable; his blue gaze is a blossom endlessly astonished by the day.

He has made plants and trees his erudition, which he generously shares.

Why devote your whole life, your whole time, your whole space, to still, wordless beings?

The Germans were occupying France when little Francis and his family fled to the country and settled there, on a plot of land in Seine-et-Marne. The parents and their six children grew plants and raised animals. It saved them. And it saved their neighbours. The war taught France that a tree that bears fruit or wood is always a solution.

Today, Francis Hallé lives part of his life on a boat that floats at the top of the forest. He sails on the roof of the world, moors himself to it without damage to study the canopy, as seen from above.

He spends his life with plants and trees. Not that he doesn't like humans, but it is true that he likes them less. He has chosen sides.

Algonquin friends have explained to me what to do should I meet a bear in the forest.

I retained two things. Above all, do not play dead. I would lack credibility as a cadaver. Instead, move away slowly, with no sudden movements, talking to the bear. (I still wonder what I would say. If I can't figure it out in the moment, I will sing.)

Backing up slowly, find a trusty tree and climb it. The bear will not likely follow me into the tree.

My friends reminded me, like an old obvious thing, that trees, for me, for us, represent safety. This should be enough to elicit our interest.

I set off into the forest with five ninjas. The night before, we watched *Kung Fu Panda*, projected on the living room ceiling. Between two uppercuts and a dragon strike, we collect pine branches. Today's class: learning what they are.

We sink into the snow up to the waist (luckily, we are ninjas today).

We return with the satchel loaded with our bristly harvest. We spread the contents of our baskets on the large table, we dry our noses and toes, and we sort through it.

Hard needles, bluish, wavy at the ends, growing all around the branch: black spruce.

Flat needles with a fine white line, set like wings on either side of the branch: hemlock.

Green prickly needles in a circle around the branch: balsam fir.

Lacy leaves, flat and broad: cedar.

And a naked branch, of the only pine that loses its needles in the winter: larch.

Long needles set in pairs that form bouquets on the branch: red pine.

Long needles set in fives that form bouquets on the branch: white pine.

Like a song to be repeated until known by heart.

The youngest takes the branches one by one out of her basket and names them: white pine, cedar, hemlock, balsam fir, black spruce, red pine. Her shining eyes eagerly gather approval from those around her.

She is prouder than when she rode her first few metres on a bike.

It is the birth of a way of speaking.

Stuck between the pages of my book, an old four-leaf clover is drying:

> Plants and rocks are covered with inscriptions in the form of veins, stria, venules, and alveolus. On the wings and shells of insects, there are figures of striking regularity, patterns that evoke the ruins of a forgotten language. There are syllables, perhaps words, definitely fragments of statement, perhaps snatches of truth. We need to do more than just be astonished by these fluttering syntagms. We need to collect them all, sort them by stamp, match them by echo, organize them by assonance, to first establish a lexicon of light, and then, why not, a dictionary of surfaces that lists every bark, every shell, every glint of light.
>
> In the slender body of its creatures, nature holds within itself the words we are missing to describe it. It is an old lesson of monks and magi and to understand it, we just have to consider it, in other words to look on it with concern and take care of it.

Such is the thinking of Alfred Russel Wallace, an ornithologist and entomologist, a friend to Darwin and fellow thinker on the theory of evolution.

The love of my life is climbing the walls. He is looking for cracks, gaps to hide in. He feels stalked, trapped. He is looking for a space where he can lose himself, but there is no more room inside him. It's full. His fingers crack, his head cracks, and the anger runs along the small surface, this house, that offers us protection. His rage and his pain stick to my feet. I can't run anymore.

I place my hand on his chest, and I try to ground him.

We cut up the pieces of the day; we create solitude for him, but it suffocates between the jaws of parentheses. The velvety light of the day stings and wounds him; he would like a burrow with no sound or light where the beginnings of silence can finally exist, the beginnings of his silence, at the end of which, maybe, he will know what he is looking for.

There are too many of us in a ramshackle house. The cold wind blows through the window that is covered with a piece of plastic crookedly cut, behind which ladybugs thaw, spinning and spinning and spinning endlessly on their backs like mad tops.

The bedroom smells like dried flies, and the lightbulb that hangs from the ceiling whines to the rhythm of its dying flame.

I flee outside the four walls to protect the loving part of me that still survives. The part my children drink from. I escape to keep it from drying up. I search for a wellspring for it. I will go back to the forest.

Along the way I latch onto a silhouette, a woman dressed in white, walking along the path. I greet her discreetly; I avoid her eyes and then regret it. We are so hungry for contact, maybe she needs mine.

When I turn back, she is already gone.

I take the little trail right behind the Blue House, through the field of milkweed.

Up above, in the densest part of the mountain, there is the one who eats raw meat with his mouth, the one with earth and dried blood under his nails, the one who speaks with his tongue. He doesn't know the words, but he knows what they taste like. He is settled in every corner of his body, and I drink from his saliva, I feed on this way of being alive.

I gorge myself on his sweat his salt his laughter that starts from the roots and shoots to the crown.

I liquefy myself alive in the pores of his earthen skin.

I spit my intensity in the middle of the woods; I grab everything that exists outside.

I am above sea level.

I breathe.

And then I come back.

And I make dinner.

I am effortlessly loving, I am a well filled again, the children drink from me, endlessly, and I pour myself into them completely.

A garter snake as long as my arm crosses the living room. I try to catch it, but it knows the house better than I do and languidly carves a path wall to wall. I am living with a snake.

It is the revolution. The five children storm the day. They are masters of the world, while the adults emerge one by one to quietly retake control of the space and the decibels.

The children serve themselves endless meals with multiple courses, make unlikely combinations of spreads, leave their finger-prints on every surface while there is still time.

You need to wait until there are enough adults to rein them in.

You need to be willing to throw yourself momentarily into the heart of the revolution.

With a coffee. And a book. It is the best – the only – strategy we have found, the adults who are the first up, to survive the violent infancy of the day.

The morning's reading therefore has particular resonance in the Blue House. It is, literally, a rescue operation.

I use my clovers as bookmarks, and they are the miniature umbrellas of the authors who are a breath of air for me. This morning, I curl up against Anaïs Nin, and she smells good. She smells like skin.

Every man brings out new emotions in her, new ideas, each relationship gives rise to a new universe. A new Anaïs.

'Every Anaïs exists only for the one who revealed her, while drawing inspiration from all the others.' I am now alone with her; I close my eyes and rest my forehead against Anaïs Nin. I want to kiss her right now.

A surprise spring snowstorm, the kind that happens all the time, unleashes itself on the valley. To respond playfully with sleds is an act of courage: no point digging in your heels against snow that covers the nascent colours, across the immense landscape.

'Come on, kids, we're going tobogganing.'

A huge yellow tractor is clearing the road. The children naturally arrange themselves as an honour guard in snowsuits and raise a mitten to the happy driver. Clark Kent, his real name. His face like an apple, his cheeks always scarlet, the little wrinkles around his honey-coloured eyes like the rays of two suns. Clark Kent is our hero. He is the arm of the record player for the land, the needle that makes the mountain sing out. He is the one who digs out the roads the humans travel along; he is the DJ of the everyday. Without him, the valley would be only wild. He allows us to be part of it.

I can't count the number of times he has come to pull me out of a snowy ditch, his singsong accent enough to warm me. If I had invented it, I wouldn't have dared make it so round and musical. Clark Kent has always been my favourite neighbour.

The children have bent branches to form imperfect circles and wrapped them in string. They have attached goose feathers, collected around Hermann's ponds. They asked me to hang them over our bed. So nightmares get caught in them. They have made a set of them.

Five of us share a bedroom. The windows don't open, but the river meanders on the other side of the plastic that is supposed to protect us from the cold, and its babble flows to us, covers the mattress and the clothes strewn on the floor.

Layers of wallpaper have been glued on top of each other over time.

They are peeling, revealing to us Mary's tastes and moods.

Little blue flowers appear under a pattern of golden stalks of wheat, which is in turn revealed under delicate pink paper. But the most beautiful, which the eye always lingers on despite having grown used to it, are the cats. All the cut-out cats that are stuck on top of layers of wallpaper, a joyful feline herd resting in its singular territory. They were here long before us, the cats standing on two legs, the cats in feathered hats, the pretentious cats, the musician cats, cats from everywhere, drawn or photographed, cut out by Mary's solitary hand. An entire wall is covered with them.

Tearing off a paw or an ear is a punishable offence. Even though the wall is falling apart, it should peel itself at its own pace.

Above the big bed, Mary used to hang some twenty strips of sticky paper on which the house's hundreds of flies came to slowly die. The flies still choose to live in our bedroom.

I spent too much time as a girl putting myself in their shoes. Feeling my wings getting stuck and my feet trying to find purchase to get me out of there. Imagining my body contort and finally fall from the ceiling to the floor, leaving a torn wing stuck high up above. I can't fly, I am vulnerable and useless: I am an injured insect.

I have given up the strips that wings stick to, and the long, noisy death throes they provoke, but the little hooks from which they hung are still there, now holding dream catchers the children made. Some dreams get caught in them and die noiselessly. But since we have never dreamed as much as we do now, I suspect the nets are mired and overloaded already.

Early each night, the children desert their mattresses and join us on ours. We spend the quiet hours tangled up in each other on the same raft; the river is rising, and the dream catcher is dripping its overflowing nightmares on us.

The damp dark of the night seeps onto the skin. I advance in the shadows; I am searching for my daughter, my little bear. The boys' voices whisper to me that she is playing over there. Over there is the rising stream. Its lively, plentiful waters, its insolent song that rings out in the night.

I call her name; I head toward the water, then into the water that is so cold that it slices through my body. My arms whip the belly of the stream, which is painfully evanescent. It is too dark and too cold. I am losing my child in the white water. I wake up in tears.

In the early morning, I hug the sleeping bodies, and I go and breathe in the start of the spring, leave my night behind me.

My phone rings.

My mother.

On the other end of the line, she asks me not to walk on the river, that it may have thawed in some places.

I stop. The sun sparkles on the ice in front of me.

My mother tells me she had a dream.

It was night. She was searching for me under the water of the stream.

Her first name means 'bear' in Russian.

Or 'the one who walks on ice' in Algonquin.

The one who sits naked among the river's jellyfish. To see what that's like.

The one who in my belly was already preparing her dragon strikes, ready for battle.

I had to stop moving because she wanted to come early, so I wrote a novel, a prisoner of my sofa, in pursuit of my grandmother who vanished. My daughter was watchful deep inside me during that time. Already strong-willed, life in a tidal wave, she absorbed with me my raw family history.

Now she lives with her emotions. She settles in, comfortably, celebrates the power of rage, honours sadness with devotion, and exalts in joy, becoming herself, wholly, joy.

When she becomes a woman, I will sometimes want to grab her by the two little sockets that I carved in her cheeks, the two dimples made to catch her. My mother made the same ones for me. It works.

My daughter crosses the frozen river; she roams the mud roads on a bike too big for her. She shouts with all her might to look out, here she comes!

I don't want her to be disappointed. I never want to whittle her momentum, completely given over to the present. I don't want the world to slip under her firmly planted feet.

'Look out, here I come!'

She runs across the road, brandishing her sword, toward the others who have already disappeared into the forest. In the curve of the dip between the hemlocks and the poplars, they have built a fort. They have hidden their provisions and invented a secret language adults don't understand.

They disappear for an hour, sometimes two, in the hollow of the forest, in the palm of our land. And they come back for lunch, starving, leaves in their hair and dried blood on their faces.

Sometimes a perfect moment then takes shape, in which impatient little bodies lay down their freedom and wash up on my loving shore.

In the curve of the road, the one that looks like a belly swollen with life, there is a new house. Which is not really a house. Which is, rather, a web of trees skillfully woven. Trees entwined, just enough to let in the wind and the stars, just enough to offer refuge.

A Japanese painter lives there; they say he is a salt harvester, that he has lived on every island, tasted their seas, and collected their white gold. I wonder what he is after here.

Before he invites me over, I watch him from afar. His skin is white and smooth. It is a break in the darkness of the forest, reflects a light that comes from within. I squint. The Japanese artist is a saline being, and he dazzles me with his light. I stay far away; I'm afraid of melting in contact with him. He busies himself around me without a glance at first.

I have never seen anyone walk the way he does. He looks like he has an invisible string attached to the top of his head, pulling him somewhere. This man doesn't linger; he moves with clear purpose, tree to tree, branch to branch, and with his large hands he collects twigs that he weaves to make walls that aren't quite. Walls that breathe and that offer protection from nothing at all.

Between these walls, he invites me to sit down.

The Japanese painter finally looks at me. His eyes take their time sweeping over me, as if they were reading the texture of my skin, the story told by my flesh.

He comes closer, and I let him. His fingers tremble slightly before touching me. His hands gently read and decode me, like a new, surprising language. They linger on the fragile space just below my neck, where the bones jut out in a shield to protect the heart. The Japanese painter strokes my skin, and my vulnerability throbs under his round fingers. I'm not afraid.

His mouth draws me in; I hide away in him. I fall.

Something in his depths is so like me. Our underground waters touch, and we form a common river, without words, in the deep.

He smells like sand, island spices, and seaweed warmed by the sun.

He holds me even tighter. With his eyes closed, his palms pressing into my stomach, he asks me to come back. He says he has been looking for me. He says he wants to paint me.

His voice is soft, but it emerges from far away. It is precious and rare.

I absorb it and steal it. I want that voice as my epicentre.

I wind my way outdoors, richer, more textured from his mystery.

I will come back.

It's a trio of mysterious apparitions offered to visitors to the Blue House, who now share, without knowing it, a volatile memory. Stories we listen to smiling, impervious. But that leave a subtle ring as a memory, a light hoarfrost, an echo that won't go away.

A long time ago, the first visitor wears a plaid shirt and jeans white from other people's plaster. The visitor is happy to work in the Blue House. He can drink his coffee while watching the birds, and the smell of damp hemlock takes him back to his native Abitibi.

He is used to solitude. He works in the city laying tiles in new condos. He is alone among new things, surrounded by people alone among new things. But being alone in the expanse of the country, well, it had been a while.

Houses from the last century creak and have an intimidating life.

He gets up at five and tears up the old boards with his bare hands. He has always refused to wear gloves; he likes to be in contact with the material. He spends his day with the material, so why not touch it.

That morning, as he goes down the stairs, he sees her. She is sitting in the rocking chair in front of the cold fireplace, gently rocking. She has her back to him. She is dressed in white.

He is scared. He flees. He will never come back to finish the job.

The second visitor is my friend. She is accompanied by her writing coach. They spend a week together thinking about a screenplay. They are fifty years apart in age, but they speak the same land: Haiti.

They set their little index cards around the living room, tracing a path of ideas through the house. Scenes are strung together, from Duvalier to the impenetrable walls of a prison, from sugar cane fields to the marbled suburbs of Pointe Claire. They are in the middle of a scene when he frowns, then falters. Facing him, she is worried. He is looking outside, over her shoulder. She follows his gaze and turns around: a white silhouette slips past them. Time stands still. A woman, dressed in white, is running around the house.

He wants to believe he is crazy; he is old and he drinks too much. But her?

The piecemeal story on the floor is gathered up: they will go reconstruct it in town, surrounded by other buildings. Where things seem more solid.

The third visitor is one who talks to ghosts. She feels it right away, she can tell right away: the house is haunted by a woman whose traces can be shared without fear. This visitor decides to move into the Blue House for a few days. She feels cared for there.

No one told her about the previous witnesses, but she leaves the countryside saying she lived with a woman in white.

While drying in my book, a four-leaf clover lost a leaf.

Does it get to keep its name despite the amputation?

Its three leaves and the absence of a leaf are at the heart of a Goethe collection.

I find the missing leaf, alone, much later in the book. It was marking this sentence for me: 'Nature speaks [...] with herself and to us in a thousand modes. To the attentive observer she is nowhere dead nor silent.'

Tree Roots. The title of Vincent van Gogh's last painting, in 1890.

The viewer can see knotty bases of trees and other twisted shrubs, almost hunched over themselves. They look like people with contorted bodies. They have tender green leaves, and the steep ground they are clinging to bursts with a sharp ochre.

There is something pained in this painting, but extremely alive at the same time. Heavy, dry trunks are supported by smaller, thin trees; the leaves seem to roll in the wind.

The painting is unfinished. Van Gogh used to set his easel somewhere near his home and paint what moved him in the landscape he spent time in every day. People sometimes criticized him for not going further afield. But he had a love for the nature right around him, for what surrounded him. He liked challenges and found it harder to extract wonder from what he saw every day, rather than the inverse.

He still had work to do on the colour and the detail in *Tree Roots*, but Van Gogh hid in the shadow of a castle and put a bullet in his gut.

Was he looking for help, for courage, by reproducing the strength and age of those trees? Or was he finding comfort in a decision he had already made?

The nature that watched him paint witnessed his farewells.

These roots were his last embrace.

Trees have great power to console.

I bring back provisions from the village and, in this morning's paper, there is an article about a man who is sorting his postcard collection to pass the time, which is moving slowly for everyone.

He has hundreds; he has been collecting for years.

His eyes look distractedly at one of them: it is from 1900 and shows a cyclist walking his bike, which has a flat tire, along a small road in Auvers-sur-Oise. On his right is a steep slope trees cling to. Then comes the epiphany.

The young collector recognizes the exact positioning of the trunks, branches, and roots painted by Van Gogh, whom he has been admiring and studying for years. The lines of the branches, their orientation around a huge trunk, are too precise to be a coincidence. This is definitely where the artist painted his last canvas ten years before this photo was taken.

After confirming his intuition with experts, the collector makes his way to the origin of Van Gogh's *Tree Roots*.

He parks his car on the shoulder of the small paved road, then walks to the wooded incline. He stations himself in front of the exact spot of Van Gogh's last painting. The mother trunk still watches over it. One hundred and thirty years later, she is still there, in the middle of the thicket, the queen of time, like in the painting. She is the last one to have spent time with Van Gogh, in 1890. Today, she greets the young, attentive collector as he cries.

I sweat out the screaming I can't do here. I slice into the air and the earth, I rip out a thick carpet of grass and young roots by thrusting my spade in the heavy soil.

I will tame the untameable and smooth the soil with my hand.

But after a few strikes, the spade hits what I at first think is a large rock. I lean over to yank it from what is protecting it. I pull it toward me to discover a rectangular stone, blackened with age. It is as long and broad as a child's back. When I run my hand over it, I find it has a name. I find a life. *Jeanne d'Arc Morency (1875–1957)*.

I have found a gravestone in my garden. I call the others.

The children wet their fingers and clean the soil-filled letters, in an already familiar gesture. They take care of the stone. They are adopting it.

Is Jeanne d'Arc buried in our garden?

Did she live here before Mary?

'Maman! There are more letters.'

Smaller, under the capital letters of her name, the children have unearthed the other part of the treasure: *wife of Royal Lamoureux.*

Names that make you want to write them.

The children bring Jeanne d'Arc into their hideout, and I go back to digging in the earth.

I am a small manufacturer of other people's happiness. I am in charge of planning, development, and implementation. It takes great patience and skill. I should consider patenting some of my inventions.

French toast with flowers, the freezing-rain Olympics, the frog battles.

In return I receive a charge of happiness, by proxy. It's not mine, but I steal it.

I try to break up anxiety and sorrow; I draw joy from the depths, even if it strains, even if it hurts.

I no longer know whether I am good or bad. I no longer know quite who I am, period.

I sculpt happiness with an axe: it is the only power I have left, and I hang on to it so I don't fall over.

The children undid the housework in fourteen minutes. The house is in carnage, and they run through it, mud-covered feet, a salamander in their hands.

My man, immobile in a shadowy corner, is yelling at people in his head.

He has withdrawn within and is waging a battle. He is attacking himself, and I know he is cruel. I sit near him, but not too near. I am careful not to fall into the middle of the battle, where I would be no good to anyone. I stay at arm's length. I stretch that arm toward him, at the end of which a hand he knows so well sets down on his sailor's torso. There is a special place for it there. A place where my hand declares armistice. A sigh. And he grows calmer inside. His yellow wildcat eyes clear. He is injured but alive.

I don't want him to die.

Class this afternoon.

Outside it is finally green.

We set off gathering.

At the end of our road, the road to the airport winds through the corn fields. The runway is overgrown with wild grass. I wonder what sort of person would land here, in the middle of the cows.

In the heart of the forest sprouts a surprising new sight, a Russian monastery, its wooden roof shaped like a golden bulb. A cemetery surrounds it: the weary gravestones, adorned with the Russian Orthodox cross, lean in the little garden, maintained by tall men in black, whose beards grow down to their bellies.

Sergueï Petroff, born during the heart of the Bolshevik Revolution in 1917, travels one day to the shores of the Missisquoi River. He falls in love with the land and builds, in this remote place, the Monastery of the Transfiguration.

The Transfiguration, in the Orthodox tradition, is the moment when Christ is transformed into the divine.

As such, the little byzantine chapel glorifies the boundary, a mysterious slash through the landscape.

Along the bank of the river ostrich ferns grow. They are rare and isolated.

You have to wait for the right time to sparingly pick their blooming hearts. One fern bud out of three per plant, no more, so as not to jeopardize their future.

We fill entire baskets with fiddleheads.

The whole family is on a mission, but the eldest in particular. Loup has emerged from his head. A new world is revealed just for him: boundless. He spots them from a distance, the ostrich ferns; he distinguishes them from the others even though until recently they were a large clump of ordinary leaves. Now they are his oasis. He heads deep into the fields up to his waist, his feet in the mud, leeches between the toes, horseflies in his hair. He finds music in the act of gathering and, in addictive ceremony, his little body repeatedly plunges toward what breaks through the surface.

We learn to cook the fiddleheads, and the gaggle of children go crazy for them: they replace popcorn on movie night.

We plant a sign at the intersection. *Fiddleheads for sale at the Blue House.* We put the precious shoots in paper cones, like at the market. Like my grandfather did on Rue Mouffetard.

Passersby detour to our remote house. They cautiously get out of their cars, which are still running, ready to bolt. Traumatized bodies, frightened at the thought of contact with another human. Throughout the exchange, a mask like a wall of paper that bruised hellos pass through. We don't linger here in the great crossing of each person. But the act is one of solidarity, and we all know that on either end of the basket new solitudes hide.

Loup welcomes the passersby with flourish. He introduces himself as the gatherer, details how to cook this new treasure. And our little road becomes a magnet.

With their presence, their smiles, even hidden, with their questions and congratulations, the passersby crown the children, who grow taller. They shoot up before our eyes, thanks to strangers who are no longer strangers.

A few carcasses of cars stop a while on the side of the road, and the travellers, bouquet of ferns against their chest, stay there. Just looking, remembering that we can be together.

Then, because they have to leave sometime, they get back on the road with their dinner on the passenger seat and the children's pride at the bottom of the basket.

I walk, my feet in the damp soil of my office, which stretches over ten kilometres, where the waves can reach me. Because there is no Internet or phone at home: the Blue House exists only for us.

Red trucks hurtle by, raining heavy nets of mud over my conversation. In front of me, an animal that I can't identify right away rushes across the road. I stop.

It is a beaver. It plunges into the ditch, letting pass another truck that is heading to the sandpit at the end of the road.

The beaver emerges again from the marsh: it is carrying a kit in its mouth. It crosses in the other direction, its baby in its mouth, running from one side of the world to the other, to reappear, without it. In the middle of the road it passes a second beaver, following in its steps: the father, also with a little one lying in its sturdy jaw.

A perfect ballet follows. The beaver parents pass each other, carefully avoiding the massive wheels of the sand trucks; they load and unload their family from one side of the obstacles to the other, where life can go on.

I count five young in all. Once the family is reunited on the ground, on the other side of the threat, I continue my route and my conversation.

I return inundated to the Blue House. It is warm, a fire is crackling in the fireplace, and my man is explaining the solar system to five children of different ages.

I settle in there, on the other side of the class, on the fringes of the scene, between twelve pairs of mismatched boots and a few crusts of rancid bread from a forgotten snack. My man talks to the children, and I see them hang on his words; I see them stretch up toward the sky. Their little bodies evaporate in contact with his ideas. Their teacher is an incandescent sun. He tells them about space, and they are in it; they become a comet, a young moon, a meteorite. They come to life, in orbit around each other, bigger and brighter than before.

I slip out.

The Milky Way lives in my living room, and my man burns at its heart.

The pink sky turns to grey and then black and flows around us. We are not submerged. A flame in hand, we shine in the dark of the night. We keep watch.

The neon city, a brief stopover.

We deposit the hard-earned money from the ferns in my eldest son's account: dozens of loose coins that the teller, who is touched, rolls as he listens to where and how fiddleheads grow.

There is a long line behind us, but the young man takes his time.

He builds little pyramids of dollars with his pale fingers with bitten nails.

He could have done anything with those hands.

He gently signals to the masked people to wait.

And he listens to the child telling him about what grows.

His gestures slow, as if he doesn't want to finish counting, as if he too wants to lose himself in the forest.

He offers heartfelt congratulations to the little boy with skinned knees who is standing before him.

I get the distinct impression that from behind his window, he envies him.

H is face hidden, my man heads off on a hunt.

Behind his mask and under the neon lights, he lines up at the street corner while I text him a grocery list.

- cookies
- bread
- milk
- cereal
- cheese

The piano vibrates with a strange 'ding.' My message appears on the forgotten phone.

Ding.
- come back

Ding.
- I want you

I am ten years old, it is thirty degrees out, I am behind thick black curtains, and I put on my wool mittens. A resonant mist has already settled over the room: the restful murmur of an audience forming. The voices mixing together, their tones naturally in tune. The bodies that house them have the same serene plan: they are attending a piano recital.

I am at the tributary of the adult world; my white water is bubbling. I feel too tall in my dress with cherries on it; my braids can't hold me in childhood.

My hands are so cold that they could fall off. I will not play the Schumann I have been rehearsing for months.

But Maman gave me mittens.

Maman told me a secret.

I close my eyes, and I rekindle it.

I am a tree. I am a tree, and my roots are strong and long. They burrow deep into the earth. I can't collapse. I am a thousand years old.

The curtain parts, I leave my mittens on a bench, and I play Schumann with all my sap, armed with my frail branches.

Today, this secret comes back to me in my body.

I am a tree when I am in pain.

I am a tree when I am afraid.

Mary never re-entered the Blue House. I think the very idea of seeing it go on without her hurt too much.

She honoured us with a brief visit just once.

She sat on the large, rickety porch, in front of Bertolt the maple, between the hammocks and the rocking chairs. She wore her blue knit, and the lace collar of her blouse formed waves around her wrinkled neck. She had put on perfume and done her white hair. She commented that the Canadian flag had been taken down from its metal pole, on which a birdfeeder now hung.

I asked her who was Jeanne d'Arc Morency, the name found on the gravestone in my garden.

'The milkweed woman,' she whispered in English, with a smile.

The children were babbling and drooling all around her.

'She was a heartbreaker … '

But then Mary put her memories on pause to follow the children with her twinkling eyes, like little miracles growing over her life.

And she says the sentence again, as if unwrapping a gift: 'Isn't it paradise? … ' Then she is off, without entering the house where her days had passed by.

A tree that is dying flowers more. It explodes in beauty, it gives it everything it has before the end, like a majestic salute to the life it has passed through. Leonard Cohen wrote that old age is an elegant way of saying goodbye. That is what a dying apple tree does. It opens flowers by the hundreds, in a final, magnificent effort to scatter, before disappearing.

In the children's hideout, Jeanne d'Arc's gravestone is covered in ferns.

Wooden swords, bowls of faded Smarties, little shiny rocks rest as offerings at its base.

Right beside it, the old barn is falling down a little more each day.

It is being swallowed up by the raspberry bushes, and its floors sag. It looks out over the Ruiter Stream, haloed in its vibrancy.

I remember the cows that lived on its ground floor when I was little. I liked going to play in the haystacks with my brother, right above them.

There were strongboxes, real or just in a dream.

From the other side of childhood, I made it a place of reverence. The barn was my hideaway and the big red cows my friends. One day, I even brought my young lover there.

Above the cows, in the dry hay, I made love for the first time.

It was quick and funny. It was like a surprise.

In the fork in the road, there is a well-known house standing in front of a string of ponds, where every year the Canada geese come to rest. They lay their eggs there, and they raise their young there. A few domestic geese joined the colony.

The weeks go by, and the goslings learn to swim, then to fly.

A fox comes by sometimes, snatching a bird as it passes: a painful protest rises up over the ponds. Then life goes on.

This existence emerges under the precise gestures and eyes of Hermann.

He made his life in Germany, in Hamburg, where he was a chemist, working for a plant that specialized in pharmaceutical research.

A life of the mind, a job between four nice, white walls, respect cultivated and well-earned. Then he travelled to Quebec and fell in love with it.

Hermann walks the roads of his new home. He finds a love, with a name that suits her: Angélique.

They settle where the mountains meet the sky. Hermann turns toward his new land. And he wants to go out and get to know it.

There are sixty acres of dense forest around their house. Red maples, sugar maples, silver maples. Hemlock, red pine, white pine, silver and white birch, oak. Deer, moose, red lynx, bears, wolverines, and even cougars, prowling in secret.

Hermann doesn't let himself be intimidated by all this life and seeks his place in it. The encounter between humans and nature can occur nobly. But it can't be improvised.

At the age of seventy, Hermann goes back to university. He does a bachelor's degree in landscape architecture.

He studies the masters: Popeau, Kent, and most importantly, Capability Brown.

A great lover of English landscapes, Capability is incompatible with the traditional French garden. In his idea of the encounter between humans and nature, there are no colourful gardens or floral ornaments. The landscape gardener mustn't be arrogant. The passage of the person who cohabitates with nature must be discreet; his hand, guided by the acuity of his eye, must tease out from the landscape what it already conceals in its whisper. Capability creates the most beautiful English gardens, from Blenheim Palace to Warwick Castle, but his work on what surrounds him is respectfully subtle.

It is written that what Shakespeare did for English literature, Capability did for English landscapes.

Hermann is the Capability of Ruiter Valley. After completing his bachelor's degree, he does his master's on his own land, applying the principles of his master to the letter.

He digs a family of ponds where he lets life take back its rights: frogs, toads, trout, herons, and the faithful Canada geese, noble signature of the landscape, which disappear as summer sets.

His wife, Angélique, collects their most beautiful feathers, which she gathers in a vase at the entrance of the house, like a seasonal bouquet.

Through the dense forest, Hermann creates trails that zigzag between trees, propelling the walker to encounter what emerges. Footbridges go over the myriad lively streams that crisscross the soil.

His trails listen, they wind, they snake, they are not straight or hurried. When you walk along Hermann's paths, something immense flows within you. A connection to the world.

A wide embrace.

An assurance that solitude is something full.

The old man manages to preserve what the encounter between humans and nature has made most moving: the space where the eyes settle without being drawn.

Now tired, Hermann no longer walks and has settled in here.

Between the forest and the marsh, he spots a bittern. This tall bird, shaped like a heron, blends into the surrounding landscape. Hermann is the only one who sees it. The old man stations himself there for hours and watches the invisible bird in silence.

One day, I join him at his observation post. All around us, the land he has moulded with such care is listening.

Hermann has late-stage cancer.

Until now solid in his dignity as architect of this place, he falters a moment. The landscape where he spent so much time becomes fleeting again, its sacred beauty catches up to him. He feels that it's his, and so close, yet it escapes him.

Hermann is searching for a way to say goodbye.

I kneel in the grass beside him.

He knows the history of the area; the name Jeanne d'Arc Morency might whisper in his ear. I take a chance, repeating Mary's words: 'The milkweed woman?'

Hermann remains impassive. 'Don't know her.'

And yet he can trace the history of this dirt road back several decades.

He knows that the Red House was the first house on the road, that it was adjoined to a small school that has since disappeared, and that all the livestock, a large herd and the main source of the family wealth, was sheltered in what is now the Blue House.

Houses definitely have a soul, an intrinsic identity, because still today, red and blue tell a bit of that same story.

I press a little: 'Jeanne d'Arc … Royal Lamoureux's wife?'
Silence.

I realize that Hermann doesn't want to know Jeanne d'Arc.

'And before Mary? Who lived in our house?'

He hesitates.

Before Mary moved in, there was a man in the Blue House who was his friend and who grew sad. One winter's evening, he killed himself. A bullet to the head.

A bullet to the head in the Blue House.

So a person can die here too.

'A broken heart?'

I don't know why I venture that explanation. No doubt because it seems to me the only one imaginable.

Hermann looks toward the field, which bows with a sudden breeze. 'She was a heartbreaker.'

A flock of Canada geese lands in front of us, on the first pond of the string.

Hermann keeps staring at the bottom of the marshland, watching.

He murmurs that, in any case, Mary's four cheerful children ran around on the floors, carrying away any crumbs of sadness that lingered.

Suddenly, his body arches and grows lighter, lifted by wonder.

He points, there, at the peak of the ponds.

'There! Do you see it?'

His voice becomes the voice of a twenty-year-old.

I look where he is pointing, but I don't see anything.

'A bittern ...,' Hermann whispers.

Hermann describes it to me like a secret: the bird is perched in the middle of the bulrushes, standing on its long legs, beak lifted to the sky. Its shape and colours melt perfectly into those of the surrounding cattails. The bittern is the master of camouflage. It blends into its environment.

Hermann sees it. I don't.

The ponds ripple in the wind, the water comes alive, the grass brushes the horizon.

The bittern undulates too. The head an arrow pointing to the sun, its lanky body moving with the fields, bending and straightening in the direction of the wind.

By my side, Hermann's aging body follows its movements.

In the Japanese painter's shelter, there is nothing but him and a small table, on which are set a few sea-salt crystals. In the morning, when the light of the day pierces through the twisted branches, he gets up and paints salt.

He says it is his way of reconstituting the original setting. The first animal that lived in the sea was a sponge. We are descended from a sea sponge. After that, the tetrapods emerged from the water to explore terra ferma. But the sea stayed within us. And we eat salt to re-establish our inner salinity.

That makes me smile. But he remains serious. And when I rest my hand on his diaphanous skin, I can feel the waves beneath it.

The Japanese painter paints like a prayer; he bows to our origins.

He tries to capture the shadow and the light that fall on the protuberances and bumps of pure crystal. He looks at salt like a new element, always astonishing.

If we are descended from the sponge, everything around us holds the possibility of an astonishing metamorphosis. Insects, birds, flowers have within them as much promise as a sponge had within it billions of years ago.

That is what the Japanese painter tries to capture.

It is my turn now. He looks at me. I know it is not me he sees, but the day and the night that settle on my skin.

He has a single brush, with a broad, thirsty tip: trying to draw detail is a trap. First he has to capture the essence, and the essence is something both specific and diffuse.

I see that he is trying to sense mine, and I don't protect myself. I want to let myself flow into him.

He looks me over with his sharp gaze. On the ashen iris of his right eye, there is a beauty mark. I didn't know eyes could have punctuation. I have found my full stop. I am ready to stop here.

I want to be the salt from the sea so I can stay immobile for a long time in this man's prism. I want to be the sole motivation for his gestures.

He embraces me; I come apart on his surface. I flow into his cracks; I join his viscera. We recognize each other; we have known each other forever. He is made of leavings, and so am I, give or take a ricochet; our blood knows each other.

He holds me so tight and for so long that I have to catch my breath. In his arms, hemmed by his light, is where he truly sees me. He can be with me only up close, where I capture no rays but his. The Japanese painter makes love to me, and new contours form on my skin.

I leave in the morning, the remains of our sighs still floating in the air when the biting dawn brushes on the table a few salt crystals fished from seas other than mine. I know that once the door is closed behind me, the Japanese painter's brush soaks up the sweat still beading on his skin, then draws the memory of my imprint on the blank canvas. Our combined waters dance at the end of his arm; his canvas drinks in the remains of our encounter. From our sweat he paints the invisible and immortalizes our secret: we love one another.

I am fourteen years old, and I am stretched out on the verandah of the Red House with my best friend. We are looking at the sky and eating a dark chocolate pie. It is the Perseid showers.

It is raining stars. We welcome each one of them like a celebration; we hide wishes in our pockets.

One day, we will live together in the country.

Twenty-seven years later: at the height of summer, the fire is crackling, and the Perseids are falling into it.

Bodies against the ground, the children pool their wishes: better to have one hundred stars for all than twenty each.

I wish I could see Santa Claus
I wish I could fly
I wish I could beat Loup at kung fu
I wish I were a frog
I wish I were a licorice tree
I wish I had chickens
I wish I could ride in the tractor with Clark Kent
I wish I could be Clark Kent
I wish I would never die

They have reached one hundred and gradually slip into sleep, confident their harvest will last.

The youngest tries to resist sleep. Clinging to the world, she whispers a story.

Lined up in front of her, a constellation of blades of grass. Small, medium, large. Some stuck together, some dancing, some curved. A family.

This child is fascinated by the nuclear family, and no other game contains as many possibilities. So she gives life to a grass family or a nail family or a pencil family. Hunched over this miniature union, she tells a story without end.

The next morning, emerging from the river, she finds a leech on her thigh.

'Hello. Do you love me?'

She grips it with two firm fingers and pulls it from her blood, which runs red down her dark skin. Then she puts it down carefully and resolves to find it a family.

Naked, her feet in the mud, my five-year-old daughter is taming leeches.

When my mother was a girl, her mother left. Two young women took her in: a small blessing with a runny nose.

Pauline and Janine. Two sisters who weren't even twenty at the time, with whom my mother shared a room on Rue Boyer for years. It was small, but there was Léo Ferré, the perfection of tomato sandwiches, and games of Scrabble.

It was small, but there was love.

I have always known Janine and Pauline as a set. Like branches of a single tree, there to stay.

Janine was an accountant at Québon and snuck home hundreds of samples of frozen treats that she kept in a huge freezer.

My brother and I would make a party of diving into them. Armed with a little spoon, we would crack the chocolate coating, chip away at it with our diligent fingers before reaching the melting vanilla ice cream and its too-sweet raspberry coulis. It was divine, and it existed only here, at Janine and Pauline's.

Pauline painted watercolours. The rolling fields of the Laurentians, the tranquil ports of the St. Lawrence, small country roads in the fog. The big sister of Marcel Barbeau, who lived off his paintings, she made them windows to another place. Walking through the hallway, you took a trip with Pauline.

Janine and Pauline were happy and lighthearted.

We would go with them to see the Québon Santa Claus and sit on his lap. We knew he wasn't the real Santa and that he was hired by Janine's company, but we pretended we believed in him, that it was true, because we liked the big room, the fluorescent lights, the noise, and the distorted radio in the speakers, beneath the giant plastic Christmas tree. We liked it because it was unique; we didn't know anywhere that did the holidays like that.

We would tear ourselves away with our battery-operated gifts, and we would stop to eat at the Harvey's on the corner. We would choose the same table and the same meal every year. Chicken nuggets with honey sauce. Afterward, we would go back to my aunts' apartment, put on our little aprons, and melt butter, which we mixed with brown sugar and cinnamon. We would spread it on our bread. It was warm, rich, and sweet.

Neither Janine nor Pauline were prisoners of their story. Together one day they chose my mother over travel, over a career, over men. My mother was spirited, passionate, and loving. And my brother and I were an extension of that.

Sitting in their living room, we ate ice cream and cinnamon butter as we cut out our Christmas list from Consumers Distributing catalogues.

As they aged, they had to leave their little apartment and move into a residence overlooking the Rivière des Prairies. From the seventh floor, they could see the ice break up in the spring.

They shared the dining room with other old people, could have their health and their hair seen to on the ground floor.

Janine would beat all the residents at Scrabble, while Pauline painted her memories. There was room for windows here too.

Janine had undoubtedly never made love, nor had Pauline. Perhaps there had been a great unfulfilled romance. That was all. They were quietly aging at the edge of the country, with ready laughs and no flashes of bitterness.

Then one day Albert arrived. He lived one floor below. A robust eighty-year-old, he had lost his wife a few years before. He had sparse hair, big glasses, and a passion for rock climbing, which he did several times a week. He was born in France and hadn't lost his accent.

Albert would go up to see the Barbeau sisters, fix a drawer or hang curtains, compliment them both, have coffee. At first it was unclear which one he was in love with. But he adored spending time with them.

Pauline, svelte and bright, a sharp, mischievous mind, was his companion.

Janine, sweet and loving, merry and warm, was his companion.

They would go for walks along the river together, a trio nearing the end of the road, allies in the last verse.

Pauline died of cancer. I was far away, travelling.

My mother had told me: 'Go. Pauline would want you to.'

I sang a Richard Desjardins song about coffins filled with black roses to kill hatred, with my love on the piano. We recorded ourselves, and my mother played our voices for her in her hospital bed.

Then one night, a call, while I was in a little restaurant in Laos: Pauline was gone.

The distance hurt more than I thought it would.

We climbed a mountain. There was a temple at the top. Between its columns I thought I would find a salve, a receptacle for my pain. I did not. It was in looking out over the horizon that I cried. There were mountains, there was forest.

I remember a bird. We give our pain at random to whatever can carry it.

I loved Pauline so much. She saved my mother.

Albert asked Janine to marry him.

There were bells and white flowers. She had her hair done, and he wore a bowtie. She said: 'I do.' Loving a man, sharing his bed, being kissed on the neck and on the tongue. Janine touched a man for the first time in her life. Hands on her hips. A new way of breathing. At age eighty.

The two hands holding one another, two pairs of eyes locked together: we carry on. Until the end.

They danced and they travelled.

When Janine started losing her memory, my mother stuck little pieces of paper on all the drawers: plates (small), plates (large), cutlery.

Sheets, blankets.

Remote control.

Albert was her guide and became the extension of her gestures, the fulfillment of her intentions.

He loved her.

Four years later, he was the one who got sick. He died in his apartment, surrounded by his four daughters and his new love.

Janine moved into an assisted-living apartment.

'Turn off the stove.'

'Bathroom light'

'Kitchen light'

'Living room light'

'Close the door when you leave'

'Lunch at 11:30'

'Supper at 5'

The walls are an automatist painting in Post-its, and their song provides the rhythm to Janine's days.

On the mirror are pictures with our names on them.

My mother visits Janine every day.

Janine starts a fire once, then twice. She has to move.

My weakened mother takes her home and ends up in the hospital because she wants to save everyone all at once.

Janine remembers nothing except her, in pieces.

She thinks Albert is the name of her electric cat, which makes hoarse meows when petted. The cat wakes up Janine in the night; the batteries are removed. It stops moving, but she still calls it Albert.

Pauline still exists in pictures, but Janine remembers her only as a child.

Janine now lives at the St. Georges long-term-care facility. With Albert the cat and her army of lady companions. She can't be alone; her legs can't grow too heavy to walk.

She trots down the beige hallways and gets the wrong room.

She steals the neighbour's dentures: 'He has such a nice smile.'

My mother writes on her walker: 'Your room is #306, the blue door with your picture on it.'

A picture of Janine smiling wide is stuck to her door.

My mother does her hair and dresses her in pretty flowered blouses when she goes to see her.

Janine beats her at Scrabble but has to wear diapers now.

The visits keep her alive. She gets out of bed and goes to the garden with her guardian angels.

But now no one can visit her. The long-term-care facility has closed its doors to the outside world. Janine stays in bed. Around her, people swarm in panic, they don't abandon her, they raise the barricades so she won't get sick. Orderlies find time to talk to her; behind their visors, they do their best to preserve what remains of Janine's memory.

We are allowed a virtual visit once a week. At the Red House, where there is a connection, we welcome her with no mask. Through the flat screen, my mother tells her about her days. She follows a list she has made so as not to forget anything, not to let her aunt down, to prevent the silence that might make her want to go back to bed.

She tells her about the owl that has made its nest in the tree, the pickles that are marinating, the Scandinavian author who brightens up the glaciers and prolongs her evenings.

We stage a little show, a few notes on the accordion, and then her great-granddaughter by way of rescue sings 'Au Clair de la Lune.' Janine is looking for an anchor. It is strange to be so close and yet so far. We can't hold her in our arms.

I shouldn't complain. But I'm suffocating.

And the shame of suffocation suffocates me even more.

Too many humans on the same floorboards.

Our time is calculated; our supplies are calculated; our days are calculated; our words are calculated; our movements are calculated.

I can't even admit to myself that I'm suffocating.

I go outside, and I see her. The woman in white running around the house. Jeanne d'Arc Morency tries to escape, but she is trapped here, in an invisible ray that ties her to the Blue House.

My father puts on old pants and a threadbare green jacket. He takes his Opinel and a basket woven from branches by my grandfather. My father is that type of person: he forgets the faces of the people he spends time with, even people close to him, but he carries certain objects through history. His memory chooses its battles.

The branches of this basket were cut in a forest somewhere in France in the middle of the Roaring Twenties. Here they are, on the edge of a North American forest, meant for the same mission: picking mushrooms.

My father walks the mountain looking down at the ground. It has been a long time since he has gotten lost in this part of the country.

Chanterelles appear like gold nuggets in the claw of light between two ferns. They are never alone. They grow in clusters.

There are the known patches, found like faithful friends after rainy days.

And there are surprises, which create real joy, so pure, so rare: the joy of great discoveries.

I like walking behind my father as he is picking.

And I like walking behind my son who is picking behind my father who is picking.

Rituals are like Hansel and Gretel's pebbles. They trace a path to the house.

They punctuate a life like little buoys that prevent one from drowning in it.

They are essential landmarks, anchors in time.

P eople are what make the countryside, and I don't know my neighbours. I pedal to the end of the road, and I stop to greet Maggie. Maybe she remembers the Morencys.

At a certain time of day, I hear regular shots ring out at her house. She shoots a gun into the emptiness. She isn't dangerous. She is sad.

She recently lost her husband, and all her pain went to one spot, right in the middle of her, at her centre of gravity. She ended up hunched, stooped as if she has been punched in the gut.

'Sit!'

She offers me maple fudge. She wants to talk.

We sit on a patch of grass in the shade, and I listen. The words seem to have been held back for so long that they fuse together and spurt out in an uninterrupted flow.

Her son has started working again. His hair salon just reopened.

Steven massages his clients' eyebrows. He knows that any form of touch counts more these days. Bodies are hungry for contact, souls are sponges.

Maggie liked having her son with her. She is gradually getting used to the solitude – it is a huge thing for her. She picks up the pieces, but she doesn't know what to do with them; she misses her husband.

She tells me how she found him, 'when the forest got him.'

Maggie had taken the little trail she knows by heart, her muffled, regular footsteps crushing the carpet of leaves on the ground.

The blind is there, a bit crooked, prettily dilapidated, like a novice stilt-walker in the middle of the forest.

'Dan?'

No doubt she scares off the animals with her unleashed voice.

Something wild pulsates in her, watchful, on alert.

Her husband is not in the blind.

She searches around it. She bends over blood, traces of blood. She smells it, tastes it. The blood of an animal, already cold.

She tracks and advances, winded, through her forest.

First she sees the fur, then the steaming red mass of organs cut up and carefully placed on the ground.

The massive animal is lying on the earth. A majestic moose, stripped down, outstretched. His head armed with antlers like a thousand rivers meeting, turned toward the sky.

Maggie takes a few more steps. Her husband is lying beside the animal.

Man and beast are facing each other.

Maggie falls. She advances the final metres on her knees, not daring to break the osmosis of the two dead, and settles as a witness before them, excluded from their circle.

The man fell on his side, a bloodstained hand on his torso. His face like a map of the world with so many ridges and valleys, still and peaceful.

Tête-à-tête with his luminous animal, he seems to have finally found himself.

He killed the moose with an arrow to the throat. He opened it up and gutted it. That was when his heart, which was so firmly attached, gave out. The inner cord snapped, and the hunter fell face to face with the animal, in the middle of their forest.

They died together.

Maggie returned through the woods. She called her son to come help.

First, they brought Dan back. His body on their backs, laden with all his memories that drip down upon them, submerging them. They lay the body of the husband and father on the big bed, still unmade from that morning.

Steven says, 'We can't let the buck rot there.'

Maggie doesn't want to leave her husband's side.

Steven goes back into the woods alone.

He drives to the animal, crushing the forest with which he is on a first-name basis. He wants to pulverize it, destroy it with the weight of his pick-up.

Winded, Steven bends over the animal.

Before loading it into the truck, he lingers on the brown eyes that impertinently reflect slices of sky.

These are the last eyes to see his father alive. Steven searches for a memory of him deep in the dead gaze.

He gets his chainsaw from the trunk and cuts off the moose's head, trying not to cry about everything that is over and everything that remains, mostly trying not to cry about all that he didn't say to his father, trying to believe that he would have chosen this death because he loved the forest more than anything, more than anyone, even him.

Maggie helped Steven hang the head of the moose that knew his father on her bedroom wall.

She catches her breath, but she's not done. Maggie holds the gun on her lap, and the more the words pour out, the more she straightens up. I see her open up slowly, so I listen some more.

Maggie brushed her mare every night. We don't know which of the two enjoyed this moment more, the horse or the human.

For the human, it was an obligatory pause. She could be fully present in her movements or, on the contrary, cast off and let her mind roam free.

Think of Dan's laugh. Of their jaunts to all corners of the forest. Of his plaid shirt laid on the ground to receive their shivering bodies, of the heat of his lips, his plant-like hands.

When she came back to the gesture, to the coarse wires that made channels in Léonie's red hair, she was calm and grounded.

For the mare it was also a moment of surrender. An entire day free in the field required of her a certain watchfulness, ears pricked toward the forest, sensors of the slightest change in its murmur.

This ritual marked the coming nightfall.

The evening moves toward us, Maggie lights a cigarette, blows smoke while watching out of the corner of her eye, and continues.

The mare's entire body suddenly stiffened, her eyes widened to reveal the red veinlets in the whites. She started to rear when a massive shadow passed just over Maggie.

An animal descended on the mare, which fled, pursued. Maggie was frozen. She wet her pants. No scream emerged from her throat. Her mare dove into the woods. Long cries of pain shattered space straight to Maggie's belly.

'Do you want more fudge?'
    'No thank you.'
    ' ... '
    ' ... '

The police took her statement.
    She told them that the massive shadowy animal came from behind. That it clearly avoided her to jump right on the mare.
    A coyote? A lynx, perhaps?

The remains of Léonie still lie scattered in the forest. The bones, the hooves, a piece of head.
    From the mare's body, they plucked tawny fur.

Maggie no longer has a husband or a mare.
    Every evening, she posts herself in front of the stable, facing down nature. A twelve-gauge shotgun in her hands, she shoots at the trees; she kills the forest that stole her loves.

The DNA analysis will show that it was cougar fur.

Felis concolor, also called a puma or mountain lion, disappeared from Quebec, at least officially, in the years 1925–1930.

Despite concerning reports, wildlife experts still don't agree on its possible return.

Before getting on my bike, I ask the now-open Maggie if she knew one Jeanne d'Arc Morency.

' … Jam … I heard about her, sure.'

Maggie withdraws suddenly; she is already turning her back on me, on her pain.

'She was too free.'

I return to the Blue House, my eyes locked on the forest that keeps its dead to itself. Shots ring out in the distance, and the heads of milkweeds fall.

We visit the grandparents in the Red House. The children are adapting better than I am to the imposed distance. They say 'bad virus' more often than 'hello,' more often than 'I'm hungry,' more often than 'I love you.' They adapt more lightheartedly to the barrier that has grown in the middle of us.

We cut branches two metres long that we hold to dance, the generations on either end of the branches. We won't let go of each other. The distance becomes invisible mortar we hang onto.

My mother is a year older today, and we sing a song about not being as young as we once were. A song that says life flows under a bridge, but the boat is still sound, and time is not idle; we will not say goodbye like this.

The music manages to pierce the grey of the days and, on either end of our branch, we follow the rhythm and sink into the ground. We are made of the same lifeblood.

There is a dancing plant.

It is called the *Desmodium gyrans*. It seems fairly common to the naked eye, like most plants. But when you sing near it, its smallest leaves start to move.

Very serious people have long been trying to work out why the *Desmodium* dances. Through what mechanism and why?

They have found nothing.

Can science detect pleasure? Joy?

Can science detect resistance?

It was summer. I had budding breasts, a patch of pimples on my forehead, and crop tops. I watched the video show *Combat des Clips*, and I was in love with the janitor at my school, whom I had ranked number 3 in the 'Big Book of Babes,' right after Keanu Reeves and the bass player from Guns N' Roses. I was in the thin-skinned, tormented heart of adolescence. I skipped school every third day because I couldn't bear others looking at me; I would hide out with Stephen King on the rooftops of the city. In the morning, my backpack on, I left my parents with the most casual 'bye' possible. I would go down the stairs that led to the alley; I would hug the walls to the street corner. There, another metal staircase climbed way up high, above the storeys, magnificently useless to anyone but me.

After checking I wasn't being followed, I would climb the steps up to the street's rooftops, of which I was queen. Here, all the houses became one long anonymous road the sky rested on, and I found shade beside skylights.

Down below, a girl with manga eyes, before that was familiar here, walked with a basket of fruit. Her beauty spilled out into the street without her knowing.

She was intense and delicious. Her vitality collided with mine.

I wanted to know her; I invited her to the country.

I had found my soulmate. We weren't made from the same cloth, but we had the same relationship with the sun and the wind.

We were thirteen or fourteen, and we were inseparable from that day on.

We crisscrossed the countryside by bike, we pitched our tents wherever we went, we danced to Balkan music in bars and fields.

One day, she went to theatre school, and I started travelling. I was going to put myself in danger to survive. Even still, we didn't lose sight of each other. We had the good fortune not to love the same boys; that spared us a lot of hurt and rupture.

She shares her days, and now mine too, with a sensitive, deep man, who is moved by things that come from the earth and who holds his anger in his inside pocket, with a little lock he sometimes loses the key to.

She is sanguine and absolute, loving and powerful. She wears an invisible second skin as a corona, which reacts to my shadows that I am unaware of. She reads me despite what I hide between my lines. And I bathe in her open book.

In this house, I feel like I have to erase pieces of me to let hers exist.

Sharing the same floors, bringing our loves together, relinquishing our hideaways, aligning our ways of being women saps us and exhausts me. The moon grows full, and we bleed together.

Territories blur; I no longer know where to hide my secrets. I no longer have trenches or areas to fall back on. Everything I am spills into the others. I am empty.

I take off by bike down the winding gravel. I devour the mountains, and I invent destinations for myself.

I need to be free, away from the eyes of the others, and to puncture expectations.

I am looking for air that is mine.

I am looking for my air.

I run away, to the edge of the monastery.

The woodsman doesn't live in the woods, but that is where we come together.

Between us, we tear up the two metres of distance that should protect us.

We butcher them, we make confetti of them, and we eat each other's bodies under a dangerous rain.

There are too many lines behind me, too many tracks that hem me in, too many edges to scrape myself on. I need space to blow them up, and this is where, in the pores of this skin, where there are no more walls and no roof, I become a leap into the abyss.

I like his large hands that fix things.

I like his tongue that tastes.

I like his solid laugh that holds him upright, like a massive crutch he has carved himself.

I like the simplicity of his relationship with the world.

He lends me his breath for a while.

As I emerge from the woods, near the exposed monastery, a giant priest pokes his head out of his garden.

He is wearing a long black robe, and his white beard falls to his knees. God interrupted his gardening to judge me.

His small black eyes follow me to my bike, waiting on the bridge down below. I jump on it and tear down the hill. I'm afraid he will follow me. It is as if he knows everything. I light a cigarette, and I leave my guilt on the side of the road. Let it rot there, alone. Or let God use it as manure. It will make his tomatoes grow.

I have a few more minutes of freedom.

My whole body hurts.

I advance through the forest. I try to undo the remaining knots.

Trees heal humans. It's a fact. In some hospitals, they planted a forest on only one side of the building.

The half of the sick people who had access to it got better; the other half died.

The forest is purple. Night falls. We wait.

Everyone in pyjamas, we watch through the window.

Then, in the distance, the sound of an engine. This is it; we all go out, excited.

Two men with stubble – father and son – get out of their truck, greet us with nods, roll up their sleeves, and open the tailgate.

'The road is in bad shape.'

We don't object. The road is mud and holes. We like it that way. We are wild.

They struggle to remove from the vehicle a wooden box with chicken wire, a little damaged from the trip. A chicken coop, heavy.

We guide them to the back of the house, to the river's edge. This is the best place to put the coop. The hens will arrive in a few weeks. We are counting the days.

The father and son leave, accomplices. They have defied the law: they are not essential services in lockdown. Moving a chicken coop becomes an illegal act of daring. In the dark of night, they leave, anonymous.

Under the red maple, the empty coop creaks in the wind.

Mice live in the house. Garter snakes and squirrels too.

We set traps; in the morning we harvest little bodies frozen in surprise.

The children find a treasure they hold hidden in the palms of their hands. They pass it child to child, moved, attentive to a life more fragile than their own.

It is a mouse the size of a fingernail. We killed its mother with our peanut-butter traps. The children tame it, speak to it in soft tones, catch worms for it, build it a cardboard shelter that they decorate with their drawings: skyscrapers, parks, cars. A town in pencil rises from their survivor's castle.

They name her: Xenia. The name of a princess for a bald baby mouse.

Xenia gets a little plate of bread soaked in milk. She is a picky eater, so she will be fed with a dropper.

The children root for her to live. They promise her trips in their pockets and undying love.

But Xenia dies anyway. To check that she is indeed dead, one of the children sinks her teeth into the animal's neck. Upon seeing her crime, the little quintet is frozen and concludes certain death.

The deceased is buried in the shade of Bertolt, who has seen so many others.

The children offer her a solemn ceremony with chocolate chips.

Kneeling in the earth, they are silent, letting the sugar melt on their tongues.

A little neighbour arrives late: the ceremony is over, the chocolate has disappeared, and mouths are dirty.

The generous children want to share their pain. Crouched around the little pile of earth, they dig the soil with their nails and find Xenia's corpse, to exhume it. They set the dusty body in the palm of the astonished neighbour, who runs to show it to his parents, triggering an absolute scandal and much emotion.

Xenia's grave is soon restored: the mouse lies in the earth, and Bertolt watches over her still.

Amen.

Little B lives down the road, at the intersection. I have come in search of butter, and he offers me coffee.

He tells me the story of his older brother, his hand clutching the steaming cup.

Big B asks his wife to go for a walk. It's time. She knows it; she is an accessory.

She goes for a walk. She looks into the distance, eyes nailed to the horizon.

Meanwhile, he swallows a bunch of pills. His movements are confident; he has pictured them often. He wants to die. The disease is stealthily taking over, one nerve at a time, like a coup. Soon he will no longer control his body.

Mechanically, he heads to the garage, settles into his old Chevrolet. They know each other like old friends. He trusts her. He has already set everything up, connected the exhaust pipe to the passenger-side window, far enough away that he can't change his mind.

He starts the engine. He puts in the Johnny Cash tape. 'Hurt.' Since his diagnosis, he has been searching for the best song to die to. He made a top five; this one could never be knocked off the charts. He closes his eyes.

He hears the voice weathered with age, the lyrics that talk about pain.

The car gradually fills with oily smoke and a hit to die to.

The song plays.

Nothing.
    And plays.

Nothing happens.
    He is not drowsy or dizzy.
    The song ends.

He is not dead.

The tape stops with an abrupt *clack*.

His wife returns.

He is upright, just like before.

Pathetic.

B calls his little brother.

'I need your help. My car's too old to kill me.'

The two brothers talk every day. They grew up together in the States, in Cleveland, Ohio. Their mother was a communist, and they hid together behind the washing machine to listen to banned music during McCarthyism.

'I'm on my way, brother.'

They live a few hours' drive from each other but have never felt far apart. They are still huddled together behind the washing machine.

When the little brother arrives, the big brother is lying down, his wife who knows all keeping busy in the kitchen. She is preparing a dose of medication that could help. The nurse has left a supply of morphine in the freezer. In case B is in too much pain.

Big B tells Little B that the nurse arrives at 4 p.m. and that he wants to be gone by then.

'I want to die.'

'Okay.'

'Promise?'

'Promise.'

Big B takes Little B's hand and thanks him. He swallows a big dose of morphine, and, together, they wait. Big B falls asleep in the arms of Little B.

The hours go by.

Little B is now sitting in the kitchen with his brother's wife. They are having a cup of tea. Lying in the bedroom beside the kitchen, Big B is still breathing.

He seems unconscious, but alive.

It is noon. Little B holds his hand a few centimetres from his brother's mouth, which is hanging open. He is harvesting his breath; his palm drinks it in, soaks in it like scarce water, endangered.

'We need to up the dose.'

Big B's wife takes out the rest of the morphine from the freezer and inserts it whole into her love's heavy mouth.

Little B holds his head. It doesn't work. He pushes with his fingers to the back of the throat.

'Swallow … Swallow, Bro … Come on.'

It works. Bro swallows.

He sinks, limp, into the bed already like a grave.

They will wait in the kitchen, door open on Big B's breathing, the rhythm of which is now slowing.

Silence… then a long inhale that seems to burst from underground. It is one o'clock, and every twenty-five seconds, there is a long, sustained sigh.

In the kitchen, Little B is going to pieces from the tension.

The nurse can't find them like this.

The wife says: 'We're going to jail.'

Little Bro and the wife look at each other.

The man gets up and feels smaller than before. He takes a pillow. He goes into the bedroom.

Behind the washing machine, the two brothers, huddled against each other, are listening to the forbidden music.

Little B advances and places the pillow on Big B's face. A moment passes. Big B jerks with a burst of life; his entire body grows stiff: he is fighting.

The little brother can't do it: this body still wants to live.

He bursts into tears.

He is angry at his big brother, who has asked him to be a murderer and who dares resist him.

He is sure he did it on purpose. He doesn't want to make it easy for him, die on the first try, just go limp and pale: no, his little brother has to be game, he has to be strong, he has to prove his loyalty.

It's two o'clock.

The big brother's breathing stops again. And comes back again, in a long subterranean rattle that flows over the silence.

'We are going to jail.'

On the wall, there are photos of a smiling Big B, a child with mischievous eyes posing by his side. Little B needs help.

He says to the wife, 'Call your son.'

The son arrives. He understands. He knew this was coming. He would not have painted the picture this way; he would have liked for his father to disappear without a trace, like a frightened bird. But his mother's devastated face. But her translucent body dragged down by fear. But the life she is entitled to as well.

The son wants to help Little B.

'I'll hold his arms.' Little B gently nods in agreement, tired of killing.

This time, he unrolls a long piece of cellophane. While the son holds his father's arms, Little B sits on his big brother's legs. He places the cellophane over his mouth and his nose. And holds it. And holds it. And holds it. And holds it. Fat tears run onto the plastic and zigzag slowly down, as if curious about this mouth that is seeking, about this constricted air.

Big B is strong. Little B is determined to keep his promise.

He holds the transparent film over his big brother's face until the body stops jerking. Until life leaves it. Until it finally surrenders.

Big B has stopped breathing.

Big B is dead.

Little B is trembling in the arms of the son, who is trembling as well. It is as if Big B's whole life is discharging through their bodies before it leaves for good.

They join the wife in the kitchen and sprawl in pain; on their knees on the linoleum, they bawl.

Four o'clock.

The doorbell.

'We are going to jail.'

They are sitting around the table, and they each open a beer, trembling. The nurse arrives.

She has comfortable red shoes, a yellowed smock, and grey roots like the first snow.

She greets them kindly, and her voice smells like filtered coffee.

She heads to the bedroom; they stay where they are.

She speaks to Big B, who doesn't answer. She takes notes. Then she comes back.

She officially pronounces Big B dead and asks his wife to sign at the bottom of the form.

It takes the wife a lifetime to sign.

The clock and its heavy hands and the son's throat that is having difficulty swallowing and the motor of the fridge and the claws of the cat on the floor and its tongue in the water dish.

The nurse hugs them one by one. Her warm cheeks smell of foundation.

Little B closes his eyes; he would like to live in the soft skin of her cheeks, drawing it over him like a blanket.

She offers him her condolences.

She stops in the doorway. A body frozen, disconnected from time. Her back is to them. And then her coffee-with-sugar voice makes its way along the ground, at floor level, so as to disturb them as little as possible.

'The morphine I left in the freezer, should I take it with me or let you dispose of it yourselves?'

They aren't sure they have any words left in them. So they look at each other and their voices help one another.

'Ourselves.'

They say it as a chorus, as if they have rehearsed it many times.

The nurse steps out of the doorframe and moves slowly so as not to scare anyone. She says, 'Good,' and she goes down the stairs with their chipped paint. She picks a dandelion in the cracked concrete and disappears forever.

Little B lives near the Blue House. He carries his story to the middle of the forest.

He spends his day moulding earth. Giving it shape, bringing it alive.

He sleeps on the verandah so he can hear the death rattle of wildlife.

Death happens here every night.

Before I leave, Little B tells me he has lost interest in the living. Except Hermann, his neighbour, whom he likes to watch from afar.

Little B looks hard into my eyes, as if he were driving a pin into a butterfly.

'But it's different. Hermann isn't human.'

He goes on, sculpting his mystery like he sculpts the earth: 'Ask Stan about your ghost. She might know.'

I thank him for the story and for the coffee, and I leave Little B in the middle of his garden, which grows blackberries and merry characters made from soil, which do not melt in the rain.

Stan lives in a pretty house, sheltered behind a bastion of tall pines, diagonally across the road from Little B.

As a young woman, she left Holland for Canada, found a job at a bank in downtown Montréal, got effortlessly caught up in the hours that run together.

Willowy and dazzling, with silver hair and a furrowed face, she now lives here, with her dog.

She came to the valley for a man. He was a psychiatrist who worked for Doctors Without Borders.

He introduced her to his forest and his house in the middle of it, and Stan never left.

Behind her house she can hear coyotes.

Every day, she walks toward them, with the man when he is there.

This vast swath of trees, stretching out over kilometres, is his.

One day, the man dies. A strange virus, brought back from a remote part of Cambodia, kills him. So Stan inherits his forest. But she doesn't know how to own land.

Stan gives her seven hundred acres to the animals.

She curls up in the middle of this new infiniteness and crawls under the fur of her old dog. A clamour rises up from the trees, muffled staccatos, that speak to her of births and deaths, and she lets herself be cradled like this in the passage of time.

She walks the forest and encounters bears, otters, mink, red lynx, and wolverines. Cougars too, and she collects tufts from their coats.

The animals' soft fur sleeps in the palm of her hand. If they are looking for territory, she will make it large.

Then Stan joins ranks with the hunters: they need protected space too, they need wildness to be cultivated. She drinks from the cambium of the forest and makes it her artillery. She sets off to war to protect what keeps her alive.

I find her here, at the edge of nine thousand acres left to the animals, thanks to her fight.

Behind her house begins the largest protected reserve east of the Rockies.

Rather than storming the barricades, Stan now heads down to the stream.

She explains that she is no longer an activist, and that she is growing closer to her heart. It's another form of combat, she whispers through a smile.

Stan removes anything that could put itself between her body and the earth.

She heads, sovereign, into the rolling abundance of her country-side. A blazing orange butterfly lands on my arm.

'Monarch butterflies can permit themselves this splendour because of the milk of the milkweed. They are the only insects whose caterpillars can withstand the plant's poison. Isn't that amazing?'

The bird that is seduced by the butterfly's great beauty and takes the risk of eating it dies instantly of cardiac arrest. The monarch is the king of the skies.

'Do you know Jeanne d'Arc Morency?'

'Yes. Sometimes she comes back with the fall. When the milk-weed goes soft.'

Stan has her back to me, but I know she is smiling.

I remain standing, frozen in the heart of the valley.

' ... She comes back? ... '

Stan has disappeared into the ferns that make up the undergrowth.

'Yes, she comes back. I imagine she has memories here.'

I am now the only person standing in this field, and suddenly I feel surrounded. Not at all alone.

I can no longer see Stan, but her voice finds me.

'Our connection to nature ... that's what will save us.'

'**M**amaaaaaaan! Come see!'

There are little white clouds of saliva all along the milkweed stems. As a child, I called it snail slobber.

My youngest puts a bit of this strange foam on her war wounds: the courageous little one, she gloriously survives the battles orchestrated by her big brothers.

In the moist warmth that reigns there sleeps an insect in the making: the meadow spittlebug.

Tiny and bright green, it watches the days and the predators go by, safe in its foam cocoon. A little bead of truth added to our delicate necklace of new secrets.

Evenings are tick inspection time. Our region is their stronghold. They are a tiny vector for a serious disease. Removing them is essential, and we have made it a ritual.

The hose of the vacuum in both hands, I suck up the flies and the ladybugs in a roar that has become a daily event.

I empty the glasses from the night before, in which a few dead or near-dead insects are floating. A dozen ladybugs tread water on the surface. Their little legs paddle non-stop. They are courageous.

I have made so many wishes on the ladybugs, and it is as if they were trying to keep my wishes afloat. There is a time for poetry: I toss their bodies in the toilet.

The children get into their big bed naked and wait for me in the shape of a star. Their bodies wide open, ready for the search. My hand runs over them like little independent countries. Still astonished at having made them. My fingers tickle backs, necks, soles of feet, looking for undesirable insects, leaving in their wake a cloud of shivers.

'Again, Maman … '

The song of the frogs outdoors, then the fireflies that claim their sky.

The generous stream at the centre of it all, jugular of the night.

A tick on my child's groin.

The insect disgusts and fascinates me at the same time. The tick is the model of patience. This one waited for my son in the forest, immobile, sitting at the base of a stem for hours, days, even weeks. Unmoving, it waits for its prey to come to it, to fall on it. If no one comes, the tick can die. It counts on others' movements for its survival. The tick can drink from the air, drawing the water hidden in it. It can sense sweat and warm blood from a distance, and animals that finally cross its path don't stand a chance.

It jumps on their skin, thirsty, and burrows in. Its head in the blood, the body exposed, it savours its oasis and gets endlessly drunk, inflating before your eyes.

I grab it, twist it, unscrew it so it doesn't leave its head in my son's flesh.

I am holding it now, its rostrum outstretched, whole and full of energy, swollen with blood and moving its legs: ready to mate.

I crush it between my fingers.

The cell network doesn't reach as far as the house. On the road, in the bend, I can snatch others' voices, which seem to come from another dimension.

On the other end of the line is agitated Montréal.

On the side of the road, daisies are about to bloom.

I pick the buds by the hundreds, in a meditative choreography, while discussing the potentially imminent release of my new film.

Two opposite spheres come into contact but don't recognize each other.

Both seem ephemeral in their own way.

The trailer will be out at the end of the summer and will run before a blockbuster.

I will buy cider vinegar in the village to make daisy-bud capers.

I climb the mountain again.

It feels good to be of no use to anyone. I am only movement. I have no other purpose than to head toward the summit. I take trails that I invent under my feet. I am trying to get lost somewhere, but I can't; all the streams know and embrace me.

I find the woodsman, my last trip. I can finally get lost here. I probe him for a long time and taste him slowly; I want to preserve his claw marks and leave drenched with his breath.

He lets me escape again for one day.

We part ways at the summit, not knowing whether we will meet again.

I make a beeline home. I am late by great fistfuls of flesh.

The ever-intact enigma of being a human is richer and more poignant when we share it with other life forms in our great family, when we pay attention to them, when we do justice to their otherness. It's about reconnecting: approaching the inhabitants of Earth, including humans, like ten million ways of being alive.

– Baptiste Morizot
Wolf expert and philosopher

Night falls after the children do.

The stars ignite, followed by the fireflies.

Learn to tame the impenetrability of the night. Our ancestral memory holds in its breast stores of mistrust, required for our survival. Advance into it. Dance with that memory.

Wake up the children.

In pyjamas, walk in footsteps we invent for ourselves. Gently invite ourselves into the immensity and accept that we are blind. Receive the warm wind that tells us where our bodies end. Walk shapeless through the night and choose to belong to it.

The children are trying to get their balance. They bend over the grass and gather fireflies, which they put in a jar.

Male and female fireflies of the same species speak the same rhythm of light. This is how they call and recognize each other. The male pulses and the female responds, their musical phrasing completing one another, and once they come together, they mate.

However, one species of firefly, the *Photuris*, has learned a score other than her own. After having played her light for the male of her own species, she emits a rhythm of light that belongs to another species of firefly. A male happy to have been welcomed joins her for the hoped-for moment, but discovers the *Photuris* is a femme fatale, and she makes mincemeat of him. From this meal, she generates a chemical that allows her to defend herself against her own predators.

The children's jar now lights their little faces from which any trace of sleep has disappeared. They slip yellow loosestrife stems and orange hawkweed into their nightlights.

I lean over what is lighting them: fireflies, little luminous beetles, generate their light thanks to a substance called luciferin.

In the night, science and poetry collide. When the luciferin encounters oxygen, a luminous pulse is created.

Over 95 percent of the firefly's energy is transformed into light: no loss of heat, unlike the bulbs that light our homes. At the tip of its little body, ordinary tissue has organized itself into an extraordinary space, capable of lighting up an entire forest.

The children all huddle under the same covers; their living nightlight awaits their sleep, which won't be long in coming.

I promised them that when it comes, I will release the fireflies.

I go out into the dark, piercing it with their reassuring presence. Millions of years of evolution in my jar, which I give up to the night, to which they belong.

My man has found a door and has passed a small part of himself through it. Gently.

Then his whole body and finally his head.

It is like a birth.

My man breathes.

Behind the counter, he juggles the dishes of a family of nine. He is a one-man circus. He drinks coffee and has outbursts of eloquence, a rain of sentences faithful and pretty, roads to this sensitive head, to his pure, fascinating depths.

My man has been saved for the moment.

I like his vastness. I like his bleeding openness and his pain. I like his intensity, his wandering reflections, his bursts of laughter, and his fingers on the old piano.

We are together now, safe in the woods at night, and we stop at a leaning tree to embrace. The air outside us is the same as the air in my body. Here, with him, I have no more boundaries. I am skinless; mine has melted into his.

The best wood is cut when the moon is hidden. It is called 'moon wood,' and it is the wood that makes the finest music. Because the true luthiers, before making a violin, first choose their tree and observe it. The relationship between the tree and the moon will determine the musical quality of the instrument. The tree stretches and its wood is honed as the moon grows. As if it were pulling it upward a bit. And when it finally shrinks, the tree's tone is restored, its wood grows more solid and massive. The wood and the moon converse, and if people want to, they can converse with them too. In the middle of winter, when the moon is in its last crescent, the luthier cuts the tree to make the finest of violins.

The second chapter of the state of emergency arrives, in which teachers and students are required to adapt and show up for new classes. Remote working platforms become the norm, and a new, arid vocabulary colonizes a portion of our heads. Since the waves don't reach under our roof, the virtual class takes shape beside the road, under Bertolt.

The setting is magnificently incongruous.

A little girl is sitting under the old black maple, which seems to want to learn with her.

She uses her sleeve to chase off flies that land on her glasses.

In front of her a computer is set on a chair.

On the screen are concentrated faces, each in their own little square.

The teacher's voice enthusiastically runs through the names of different shapes. Rectangle, circle, oval, octagon …

Around the house, other children do battle with broad swipes of branches.

In the vegetable garden, the adults stir up the earth and straighten the fence.

The little girl drinks in the new words like water, drawn into this tiny square of knowledge.

Behind the insects, she thrusts her hand in the air: she knows. She knows!

We cut birds out of a book with pages yellowed with age. The little hands carefully cut around the fine head of the yellowhammer and the dorsal curve of the peregrine falcon.

The birds are so precisely drawn in the book that they seem alive.

Gould, the master behind their perfect portrait, is a nineteenth-century British naturalist. He was among the first of the ornithologists.

John Gould, like his contemporary John James Audubon, travelled the planet by boat, with hundreds of men in his service, to sketch the egg-laying world.

A perfect portrait normally requires at least one hundred specimens as models.

Killed, dismembered, reconstructed for the pose. Taxidermy work is necessarily long, such that the portraitist often draws the first line surrounded by the intense smell of rot.

Their disciple, Tom Harrisson, grew up in the country. He spent most of his days collecting winged beasts.

Dragonflies and damselflies first, which he kept in matchboxes.

Then birds, which he captured and placed in a little aviary he built himself.

There he spent hours observing and drawing them.

In his early twenties, he hunted down a magnificent bird in great demand with milliners of the time: the great crested grebe. He published a long article on his observations in the prestigious journal of the London Natural History Society.

But the death knell tolled for avian massacres at the end of the nineteenth century. In Great Britain, the Plumage League rendered the art of taxidermy obsolete. The occupation of naturalist scholar as it had been practised and recognized to that point died out.

If it was no longer possible to freeze the living to observe it, then we would have to learn patience.

Tom decided to blend into the bittern habitat.

To put himself at the level of the bird.

For him, it was not simply a question of identifying birds by the colour of their plumage. It became a question of meeting them. And for this, he had to become a bird, observe its exploits and movements and note them, scrupulously and without judgement.

So Tom spent his days on his knees in the marshes becoming a bittern.

But he was barely earning a living. He reluctantly tore himself away from his rural life and found a modest house in a disreputable neighbourhood of a small industrial town, where he searched, in vain, for work.

Everything around him seemed sad and grey. Except the living.

At the beginning of the 1930s, Tom formed the group Mass Observation.

Since he could no longer observe birds, he would observe humans.

His idea was to found a 'science of the masses' through the large-scale collection of data about the day-to-day lives of people.

He slipped into taverns, alleys, and factories. He observed other people and noted, as scrupulously as he did for birds, their exploits and gestures. Still without judgement, still with vivid detail: words, songs, gestures, demeanour, clothing, and interior décor. A technique adapted from the one he used with the winged ones. Tom became the others. He spent hours in the local pub, filling in the pages of a notebook: in it we can meet old toothless men, know what and how much they drink, read the content of their conversations.

The archives of his investigation, *The Pub and the People*, are witness to an otherwise invisible proletariat fauna.

Tom's Mass Observation to date contains over three thousand reports from the field, where the behaviours of human animals are observed, in the detail of colours and movements. Tom Harrisson, to my mind, is one of the first documentarians.

On the tips of their toes, lifting their collages to the sky, the children adorn the Blue House with portraits of birds so fine that they watch us.

Our long-awaited chickens finally arrive. There are five of them. Each one baptized by a child. Tigresse, Roussette, Poco, Lila, and Gourmandise. They are skittish at first and don't come out of the coop.

Then, little by little, they venture out into the yard, even come in the house.

They aren't laying yet; they are too young.

They let themselves be petted and chase butterflies.

One morning, a piercing scream rings out. It is coming from the verandah. In her little tent, the youngest member of the expanded family screams, terrified. I run to the nook of the child, who normally uses this as her place of ultimate refuge, escaping the horde of people bigger and stronger than her.

She is shaking like a leaf and holds the note of her scream, still piercing, sitting in the tent facing a chicken that seems as panicked as she is. Neither of them is moving, both frozen in a territorial stand-off.

I take the little one in my arms; she can't stop crying: her *Frozen* blanket has been colonized by the chicken Gourmandise, which cackles with panache, refusing to cede her place.

I struggle to get the chicken out of the tent; she resists, having settled in.

And I discover an egg, round and warm, on the chest of blond Elsa.

Our first egg, laid on the fake velvet *Frozen* blanket. Gourmandise will no longer want to lay anywhere else.

'But it's my fort,' the little one protests, and rightly so.

We hide the tent, but Gourmandise searches for it everywhere, desperate.

The coop seems too conventional for her.

Seeing her like this, searching for a place that suits her vision of laying, is upsetting: we take the tent from its hiding spot.

Gourmandise walks around it, dissatisfied.

The little one raises the obvious in the midst of our noisy questioning: 'She needs her blanket.'

Obviously.

While the child looks on, resigned, the adults set up the synthetic nest for the hen.

Finally, she rushes in and curls up comfortably. She lays again, a warm egg in her castle, under the whisper of her ally who understood, before the others, the need for a foxhole.

I look for one of my own. My foxhole, my retreat, my hidey-hole, my salvation.

I pedal to the bend in the road to meet the Japanese painter. I want to swim in his waters that know me. I want to drink him up even at the risk of drowning.

But his shelter has disappeared. There is no trace of the trees he used as a shell. Nothing remains but a pause in the forest, a little circle cleared of its trunks.

The painter has left, with his smell of the open seas, with the little tender space behind the ear where I felt like I came ashore, with his arms that broke through my dams and his beauty mark deep in his right eye. He left with his brush to collect essences other than mine.

Between the trees an island remains: a white, wavy canvas. The traces of our sweat combined. A canvas swollen with the salty memory of our embedded bodies.

Around the vegetable garden, the grandparents are growing full bushes of wild roses. Grand-Manon makes the best jam with their delicate petals. But they are under siege.

The children are called in as reinforcements: they are to hunt the Japanese beetles that hide in the flowers' crowns. There are hundreds to kill. The children get to work, diligent and concerned.

They crush the orange insects between their strong little fingers, not without some pleasure.

Observing the beetle he has placed in his palm, the youngest boy reflects.

Who decided the fate of this insect? Who decided it is a pest?

He is philosophically opposed to the power conferred. There are no bad insects, just as there are no bad plants – a theory that has so far gotten him out of weeding the vegetable garden.

He is right. It is all a matter of perspective.

Yet he crushes the insect between his fingers.

He is compliant this time, but only to save the jam.

Evening comes, the sky is purple: it is grappa hour for Grand-Papa, who settles in outside, his pellet gun on his lap.

The children drink hot chocolate in silence at his side. They wait.

Something moves. The eldest points: a chipmunk has slipped into the chicken coop and is eagerly dipping into the trough.

Ready, aim, fire! Bullseye!

The chipmunk is lying on the ground, its legs pointed to the sky, its cheeks still stuffed.

The children will bury it with the others. Death is easier to take with full cheeks.

In the trailer behind the tractor, a mountain of twigs, brambles, and dried grass.

At the wheel, my proud son heads toward the field to unload the debris. We will make a bonfire.

The younger ones run and then jump in the trailer, make a nest on wheels in the midst of the dead branches. The nine-year-old driver carting a load of small humans encounters Clark Kent at the wheel of his red tractor. On either end of life, each in their own language, man and child wave a companionable hello.

Crouched at the end of the garden, which is growing magnificently wild, I wonder whether the body of Jeanne d'Arc is feeding this fertile land.

Clark Kent approaches. When the tractor engine cuts out, it is like part of the valley has stopped breathing.

'Morency?'

He thinks, scrolls through the bit players in his memory, hesitates.

'She was special.'

He knows.

'She gave me my first job.'

My hands black from the soil, I now hang on Clark Kent's lips, as he sits on his metal throne.

'We used to call her Jam.'

Jeanne d'Arc didn't want to rest, when, on the other side of the world, men were dying. She wanted to go to war. 'It was the end of the summer, in 1940, if I remember correctly.' Jeanne went out into the fields.

She hired all the children in the county. 'We became her little soldiers.'

From dawn to dusk, Jam and the children picked. They filled baskets with milkweeds, extracting their silk.

'You know, the soft part of the plant?'

Clark Kent rubs his thumb on his index finger, the imprint of the gesture, the resuscitated memory of past harvests.

Then the myriad little harvesters followed the lady to the house where they plucked the soft part of the plant and then sewed, until daybreak, life jackets that would be shipped to the Allies.

I can hardly breathe. The fabric of humanity takes my breath away.

Clark Kent pauses. He says that he never knew whether their efforts helped any, or even whether their life jackets were sent to Europe.

'I could get into trouble when I was bored … She kept us busy.'

His small eyes squint, and his voice drops down to the ground to meet me. He is going to tell me a secret. I move in toward him.

'She was a rebel, you know … '

She made bows out of milkweed stems. 'It was illegal for women, and dangerous for me. But the world was falling apart, and we were alive.'

Some nights, the children, hands still sticky, returned to the fields with Jeanne and the women she had convinced to come out of the kitchen. And together, they split the sky with their arrows.

'Up to the moon … '

Clark Kent stays there for a while, on the moon with them.

'Sometimes rules are made to be broken.'

Then he turns the key to his tractor as if to get his breath back. His scrap-iron armour trembles. Clark Kent comes back to his life.

I shout over the noise: 'I found Jeanne d'Arc's gravestone, right there, in the yard!'

He doesn't seem surprised.

'Yeah, those stones were solid enough to hold up houses,' and people 'borrowed' them from the cemeteries to shore up their foundations. They are all over the region.

Clark Kent waves to me and disappears at the end of the road.

So Jeanne d'Arc Morency's grave was the foundation for the Blue House.

We have been held upright so far thanks to her.

Clark Kent has always been here. He is part of the land.

He exists only in movement: his tractor is his shell, set on his broad shoulders. Clark Kent crosses the fields, armed with his large shovel and his forthright smile. He straddles the seasons on his metal beast, fishes from the depths of winter cars disappeared under the snow in his valley, as he would remove an eyelash resting on a cheek: in a smooth, delicate gesture. His tractor is a natural extension of him. He digs the ditches and tames the stream swollen after heavy showers.

At the sound of Clark Kent's tractor, pure, deep joy takes hold of the children, who line up to applaud their hero.

One day, Clark Kent's house burns down. All that is left is a pile of black ashes surrounded by a few cows and carcasses of heavy machinery.

His wife leaves the road. She will live a few kilometres away, where the asphalt begins.

The tall, quiet man, who can build anything, does not erect a new house on his land. Sometimes he sleeps at his wife's, but often he sleeps in his tractor, his shell.

The children think he must eat screws and bolts to be so strong.

One unremarkable evening, the night blankets the valley, but Clark Kent is nowhere to be found.

His wife is looking for him. The wide tracks of his tractor lead into the woods, where he is used to working. His wife follows them like friendly prints; she knows their contours; she knows their path will lead her to the man she loves.

The engine hums in the distance: Clark Kent is still working, splitting robust trees into logs.

His wife approaches but sees only the tractor's empty shell.

Beside it, the knife-like splitter is running. Two mechanical animals in conversation. The sharp blades of one of them slice up the earth and a confetti of wood flies into the night. A confetti of flesh as well.

Clark Kent fell into the beast, which swallowed him whole.

His wife's scream is still stuck in her throat.

Clark Kent's tractor lost its heart and rusts, immobile and disembodied.

The children didn't cry. They didn't speak either. There are times when the voice goes away. They draw Egyptian gods with dog's heads and human bodies. They glue flowers to them and write: 'Clark Kent I love you a lot.'

The storm rolls in slowly, as if it were part of the story. We sit in clusters on the verandah and wait. It bursts right over the house. The lightning fills the sky, regal and violent.

The children relinquish their pain to the tips of the lightning bolts.

That evening, they are afraid of the storm and of death. They face the great brutality of life and see its magnificent unruliness.

They will have to resign themselves to it.

I take refuge in their flesh and their untameable fears.

A secret makes its way to my belly.

'Maman, when you die, I will bury you under my bed.'

The next day, we decide to break the rules. We close our eyes and open our arms: we collect backwards hugs from the grandparents. An embrace filled with all those we have missed. My mother washes up on the backs of my little ones like on an island in the midst of a storm. Rescued.

This time, they cry. The closeness brings up those who are missing.

I would like to make poems out of real objects. The lemon to be a lemon that the reader could cut or squeeze or taste – a real lemon like a newspaper in a collage is a real newspaper. I would like the moon in my poems to be a real moon, one which could be suddenly covered with a cloud that has nothing to do with the poem – a moon utterly independent of images. The imagination pictures the real. I would like to point to the real, disclose it, to make a poem that has no sound in it but the pointing of a finger.

– Jack Spicer, poet, to Federico García Lorca

Nineteen forty-four. A boat pitches on the murky waters of the Channel. Its split side creaks as the iron wound expands: it has been hit, and it is beginning to sink into the inky depths. Dozens of panicked bodies are running around the deck. From a bird's-eye view, they are all the same: billiard balls on a table being tipped. They run in every direction, bump and collide, then roll toward the water that, with a heavy tongue, swallows them.

A surviving hand, which the rest of a body hangs on to, clutches a life jacket.

The man gets it on just before a wave carries him off.

The man swallows the brown water. He will have a bit of this colour in his eyes for the rest of his days.

The distant shore does not seem any calmer than the water, which continues to swallow bodies.

He is floating. Breathing. He places his hands around his body, hugging his life jacket, erecting a dam against fear. He doesn't want it to seep into him; let it storm everything else instead. He is floating.

Jacques, who will become my grandfather, will stay in the water for hours, maybe days. When all the other bodies have stopped moving, he finally decides to swim for shore.

He avoids the fallen men and their twenties suspended for all eternity.

He walks to a tree, a sycamore, which will witness his rescue.

He falls asleep there, still protected by his life jacket.

When night falls, he finally leaves, with a step that will forever be heavier.

Under the sycamore, the abandoned life jacket bears a label sewn by the hand of a Canadian child. Three letters as an epigraph: JAM.

In the river up to his waist, my eldest is searching in the water. Bent over, he scans the moving depths. He is serious. A bag on his shoulder, he is collecting rocks. They have to be flat, round, and thin.

He spends hours like this, bent over all that shines at the water's bottom.

Legs red from the cold, his satchel full, he finally comes back to the house, where he goes about wrapping his rocks in a single, large package, which he will give to his teacher, whom he hasn't seen for months.

When he thinks of her, the pain against which he has erected a dam overflows.

Her name cannot be mentioned, as the risk of a flood is too great.

This young teacher has understood him. A divining rod, she filled the persistent void that spreads inside him like an ink stain, indelible.

The year brutally interrupted has deprived him of this deep, still nascent connection. So without saying much about it, he sets about inventing a tailored gift: a bunch of skipping stones.

We will go to Montréal so he can give them to her in person.

In the distance the rusted carcass of a tractor vibrates as it advances lazily.

Wendy, Clark Kent's daughter, is at the wheel.

She has his eyes, and palms as big as the local forest.

That evening, my son's delicate hand takes the raw, sensitive hand of his father. And brings it to his chest. In a mirrored gesture, it is the child's turn to cover what is swallowing him up. To settle the chasm and soothe the void. Nothing to say. It all happens there, abyss to abyss, from one anchor to another.

I turned over the soil listening to Johnny Cash, then I planted lots of cucumbers, because we love cucumbers.

At the season's end, I harvested enormous squash, lots and lots of squash. But no cucumbers.

I am starting from scratch.

The children make a salad with what they have learned to name and taste.

- wood sorrel
- purslane
- plantain
- nettles
- violets
- musk mallow
- stonecrop
- galium
- blue-bead lily
- bergamot

We also uprooted a large burdock in the rain with our shovels, and we opened it up and extracted its hearts. It was hard work, and it didn't taste good.

We learned the song of the veery, which flows like a river on the mountain at night.

Also the colours of the white admiral, the tiger swallowtail, the Milbert's tortoiseshell, the summer azure, the northern crescent, and the viceroy, which resembles the monarch.

Many butterflies gather pollen from only one species of flower. Even if another, nearby, offers a better meal and makes them stronger, maintaining their connection with their flower better ensures survival of the clan, because knowledge of this flower is passed on through the generations.

Scientists have called this connection *flower constancy*. It is not practised by all pollinators, but many honeybees, bumblebees, and butterflies maintain a unique connection with their flower even if it gives them less in the short term. Over time, the language, the finesse, the habit developed between the two makes the species stronger.

Behind the Blue House, the milkweed flowers that feed the monarch caterpillars become orange, now decorated with magnificent, deadly butterflies.

We pick the flower buds of the plant, which we boil twice. We eat them like broccoli. They're a little bitter and very tasty.

I encounter a pure pride here, unrelated to ego. I start to recognize what is around me. Because we often associate joy with children, I first thought I had woken up a dormant child inside me. But what I feel is not exactly joy. It makes me stronger.

A whole swath of my humanity awakens, like a continuation of myself, an extension of a woman, suddenly in conversation with the rest of the living world.

I feel like I am spreading out. I am no bigger or stronger.

I am simply more vast.

Seven o'clock. I am teaching class today.

I get up. The children are already downstairs, cereal covering the counter, the table, and the floor: it is an open bar, self-serve.

I avoid the chaos, plunged in Romain Gary: *Do not describe things as they happened; make them legends.*

Like my mother and the ambulances. I know how to grab reality by the scruff and magnify it.

The children will soon be ready for their second course of breakfast and, before I'm hit with multiple requests, I put down my book and open the door to the field. I never grow tired of this picture. The fog is snagged on the mountaintop, goldenrod season is beginning, the first stirrings of fall.

It smells like the burnt wood of a fire dying in the distance. The rising sun warms the earth, which is sweating off its night.

I grab a towel, as I do every day, and I head sleepily down to the river. This is the start of my day, my daily dip, and it is worth ten espressos. I undress and slip a foot in the mud, then my whole body in the icy water. I open my eyes under the water to look at the sky. I like seeing it from here.

Something brushes my leg. It's big. I pop my head out of the water. A beaver is staring at me.

Neither of us moves. He is in my bubble, clearly. And I am in his. Neither of us yields. He doesn't seem scared. He dives again near me and brushes against my bare thigh. I dunk my head in the water and search for him. I swim slowly and now we are face to face. In this moment, I could take his place. Live there on the edge of the current, make it my home. Live between the walls of woven trees and the clear basin of the stream.

Since I have a hard time picturing him making toast for the children, I decide to get out. I am shivering. Wrapped in my towel, I see him burrow into the shelter of the rock. I think you might say we have met.

I head back to the Blue House luckier than when I left.

The earth trembles and the sky is pink, a coup and its repression waltz in the living room, and I take refuge in reading *The Nature of Things*.

It is as if he has always been old. In all his photos, Francis Ponge has a grooved face with eyes that are troublingly, invitingly black: a gaze with many paths, an intelligent gaze.

He should have been more celebrated, but his era placed him in unfortunate opposition with his contemporaries, Jean-Paul Sartre and Albert Camus.

They found themselves assailed, attacked by the plurality of the world that confronted them. They couldn't name it, and they consciously refused to try. 'A tree is a life wasted, like insects on their back that can't get up,' said Jean-Paul Sartre, who openly hated everything that lived outside him. In *Nausea*, trees are 'soft monstrous masses, all in disorder – naked, in a frightful, obscene nakedness.'

Sartre and Camus focused brilliantly on humans and their inner battles; they decoded their landscapes and chasms and placed that land above all others. But the Outside World became a monolithic block that they refused to describe.

'Mamaaaaaan? Mamaaaaaaan?'

The toilet is clogged, the little one has taken a bite of soap and is blowing bubbles, two mice are caught head to head in the same trap, dying while looking each other in the eye.

I stay the course, my day hasn't started, I remain focused on my reading.

Ethnology, sociology, history, philosophy, politics, and psychology speak only of humans. The words exist, though, and the mission of the person who wields them could be to place them on what surrounds them. That is what Ponge tried to do.

Vertical channels open within the bark, and through them moisture is drawn down to the ground, drawn to lose interest in the vital portions of the trunk.

The flowers are scattered, the fruit is dropped. From a tender age, the relinquishing of their living attributes and bodily parts has been a familiar exercise for trees.

– Francis Ponge
'Trees Coming Undone Within a Sphere of Fog'
The Nature of Things

Acting as a sentinel, Ponge resisted the currents around him.

While the others abandoned the detail of nature, he looked at the scrolls of a shell. He tried, for better or for worse, to accurately describe what existed outside of him.

The children open the door to go outside. I say: 'Not near the river.' They say: 'No, we promise.' I get up, settle in on the verandah so they exist out of the corner of my eye.

Albert Camus congratulated Ponge for his poetry: 'I think *The Nature of Things* is an absurd work in its pure state – I mean it is born [...] in the extremity of the non-meaning of the world. It describes because it fails.'

Francis Ponge replied, shocked, misunderstood: 'Of course the world is absurd! Of course the world is meaningless! But what is tragic in that? [...] If I have a hidden motive, it is obviously not to describe the ladybug [...] but to not describe man. Because: 1– people go on about man far too much; 2– etc. (repeat ad nauseam).'

'Maman, look, who's this?'

My daughter has encountered a new insect. Grey, flat, oval, with many legs.

I called it 'termite,' not knowing why. In the huge category of common, ugly insects, who are saddled with a name not their own.

But this insect is a miracle. It is a member of the crab and lobster family. It is called a woodlouse and is the only terrestrial crustacean in the world. It has seven pairs of legs and two pairs of antennae.

Its ancestors lived at the bottom of the sea. Maybe partially in their memory, the woodlouse has blue blood.

With Ponge, animals have souls and streams have rights. Yet, the voices of Camus and Sartre prevail, not his. To say that we still live in the shadow of this defeat would not be an exaggeration. As arts and science grow more distant, the lexicons and the colour charts grow impoverished. Should we be surprised that the oceans and our stories are being depopulated at the same rate?

– Romain Bertrand
Le détail du monde

There are always five of them, clumped together in front of the river. The two brothers pass the fishing rod back and forth. Small brown trout gleam under the lively foam.

My youngest wants to swim. They negotiate five minutes. Five minutes when the fishing rod is removed from the river; five minutes when the little bodies plunge into the cold water; five minutes when cries and laughter explode. The beaver will keep his distance, a witness to the pulse of life, too dense to get entangled in. The shivering children emerge from the water. The eldest drops his line again, concentrating on the fish that don't take long to return. The five children, still naked, grow serious. They wait patiently, almost in silence. A bite. Triumph. A shiny brown trout wriggles in the air, then on the ground. The children scream to the whole world that they have a fish. 'WE CAUGHT ONE!'

Their little hands squeeze the animal's resistant body, tear the hook from its mouth, grab a rock and hit it once, twice, three times on the head, which opens and bleeds.

They all share the act and its violence. They all observe the animal's death, which takes its time coming. They all see the life that holds on, then suddenly disappears. Nothing left.

A small bloody rock in the hand. Five little naked, silent bodies, coming back up to the house, the weight of a life in a palm of a hand.

Between sadness and pride. They have caught dinner.

The woodsman has a wife.

She is beautiful, deep, and alive. She gives me a plant to put in the soil.

My vegetable garden is full.

I refuse to let something of hers take root at my home.

I let the lonely plant die quietly at the entrance to the garden, where the rest blossom without it.

The days pass, and its leaves slowly turn yellow.

The children found it. The plant's leaves are drooping, but the roots are still willing.

I grab it with one hand; it is frail and could die now.

I reluctantly find it a place, between the sunflowers and the tomatoes. I dig the earth, place the fragile plant, spread out its root base, bow before the beauty of the woman who gave it to me, and cover it up.

The children apply their little palms all around it. They ask me what will grow at the end of the leaves.

'Maybe nothing.'

'But if it survives?'

I look at the limp plant, laden with history.

'If it survives, a chili pepper.'

I don't know what I will do if fruit grows at the end of this unwanted plant.

The sound of Clark Kent's tractor resonates in the distance. The children run toward it, freeze beside the road, their eyes turned toward the still invisible tractor.

They are silent, balanced between two emotions. There will be tears and a knot in the stomach for the loss of Clark Kent. There will also be a burst of laughter and burgeoning joy for the next chapter in the story. They are beautiful. They stand there together, not choosing which side to take. They are five little tightrope walkers, both sad and happy, their arms raised to the sky on the side of the road. The honour guard takes its place again.

The tractor arrives, with Wendy at the wheel.

And they applaud when she waves to them as she passes. Wendy doesn't slow down. Later in the story, she might, when the curtain of tears that overflows from her eyes has parted. For now, she tries to befriend her tractor, her road, and her new life.

I find sweet clover on the side of the road. It is like finding white gold and, suddenly, I see it everywhere! Hundreds of white flowers, like little fingernails perfectly trimmed in half-moons, arranged haphazardly along the stems, in a seductive chaos, with the unique smell of pepper and honey.

I announce it to my son as if it were big news. Which becomes bigger when he receives it. We share the excitement of this discovery. We head off along the roads where suddenly thousands of bouquets of our precious boreal vanilla are blooming.

Sweet clover, which was used by Indigenous peoples to perfume milk, cakes, compotes, and bread, has fallen into obscurity. It grows on the side of the highways and is the first weed clipped by the mower.

My son hugs a big bundle to his chest.

Together we enter the landscape, in an improvised but harmonious choreography. We get blisters from gathering.

Our ambition fills the trunk of the car, open like a giant mouth.

We travel in a cloud of wildflowers listening to Ella and Louis sing 'Summertime.'

We spread our spoils on the table, and we make large bouquets, which we hang in the sun, head down.

Dried sweet clover everywhere in the house; its fragrance settles under the skin.

A white van stops in front of the house. Who has ventured here, to the end of the road?

I go meet the person while watchful little heads take position at the window.

A young, jovial man smiles at me from beneath his company cap. A crude drawing of a beaver on it. Above it, in block letters: 'Beaver Control.'

'Can I help you?'

The young man is looking for a dam to dismantle. Beaver dams make the water rise and increase the risk of flooding. It's the season.

I step back, look at him in his immaculate Beaver Control truck, and I place him among the bad guys.

'Do you kill them?'

He almost shouts at me, insulted that I would ascribe such intentions to him. Of course not! He relocates them! His cheeks are flushed with emotion at the very idea of hurting them. He explains that he dismantles their house, branch by branch, and that the beaver family, finding itself homeless, is captured in cages – which are very comfortable. He takes them further away, where there is less risk.

'The family?'

The young man with round cheeks and dark eyes looks like a beaver. He goes on, excited by my questions, happy to share his passion with me: 'Yes, beavers are monogamous and mate for life. The family is the base unit of beaver colonies, and the female is the central figure in them.'

Here, he pauses as he devours me with his eyes.

I become a central figure.

I break this strange silence by telling him there are definitely no beavers near our house. He looks at me tenderly. He is no fool. So we share something. A love for this impermeable creature, which we used to make hats from.

For every beaver caught over here, eighteen hats would be found on European heads over there. For a family, almost one hundred hats.

Kilos of silky fur ripped from the twisting white water to find themselves promenading at Montmartre.

The gentle beaver-control man smiles at me, complicit, and continues on his way.

A few air bubbles rise in the stream below. A sigh of relief.

Surviving with nine of us in our old house.

Sharing rhythms, tastes, territory, and desires. Meeting everyone's needs except one's own. Cutting up one's freedom, not knowing what to do with all the pieces. Swallowing them, choking on them, and being ashamed to complain, belly full.

I visit the mountain hermit.

He lives alone, far from the road. People say he fled to tend to his broken heart under the white pines.

In the middle of the woods, a small shelter, solid and effective. No coquettish touches here: four walls and a roof. Toïvo is tall, strong, and handsome. He has a white beard and hides his hair under a Viking cap, decked out with two genuine horns that gleam in the sun.

I am astonished by the power of love. What else could make such a large man run? Or is it the battle against this immovable pain that made him a giant?

Toïvo stumbles. He admits with a solemn voice that he has been drinking and will carry on doing so, because today he has to slaughter his cow. The massive animal looks at him as if she knows.

Toïvo avoids her eyes and justifies himself: he has to eat and get through the seasons.

A few times a month, a neighbouring family leaves him provisions at the base of the mountain. A basis for survival, which he goes down to fetch and places in his fridge. His eyes shine, and he looks at me for the first time. Yes: he made a fridge, and his pride momentarily casts a shadow over his pain when he demonstrates.

A cylinder of shelves drops into a deep hole underground. Toïvo pulls it out using a crank. The food on the shelves is conserved by the coolness of the earth.

Just as ingeniously, Toïvo has placed a windmill in the river that runs along his home to generate enough power to run a homemade washing machine.

Toïvo is a hermit who smells good.

His large hands run confidently over the inventions. Needing no one but himself is his salvation, his response to such a massive wound. A question of honour and a way to have the last word.

Plus, he is not alone. His vast arm embraces the canopy with a grateful gesture.

He offers me a swig of vodka before emptying the bottle, then asks me to leave.

Now he has to kill his last friend.

I leave him that way, a mountain giant, immense and courageous.

A shot makes the trees shudder and their leaves shimmy.

I learn a few weeks later that he is gone. The forest lost him. Though he made a place for himself as a perfect hero in troubled times, nobly resisting the passage of time, he went to live in the mouth of the wolf, in a retirement home, where it is written that we must end our days.

Now he is hall neighbour to Mary. The Viking and the Ukrainian, the king and queen of the valley, dine side by side in the little beige dining room, the windows of which look out over the parking lot. They don't talk much, but they look at each other sometimes. They have not given up.

They know the mountain and the white pines and the river and the wind and the forget-me-nots.

They will go back there one day.

I let myself be sucked into the forest.

I feel like I can belong to this surface. The space between two streams, the curve behind the rock that looks like a face, the tongue of land that leads to the summit.

I become porous to what moves, to what trembles. It is not my head that it interests, it is my blood.

The damp, sweet smell of the balsam fir, the earthy, concentrated smell of oak. The perfectly punctuated dance with the sensitive fern, appropriately named – a lacy fern that waves top to bottom, elegant in its embodied breaking with immobility.

Everything is at once so fine and so generous. I let myself be swallowed up.

There is no longer skin between me and the trees.

I sit on a dead tree, torn from the soil during the storm. The mountain is striped with these mighty gashes, monumental scars from the quiet rampages of recent days.

A forest with no straight road is a happy forest. It is flourishing if one has to zigzag between its trees and the dead trunks that make other lives possible. Salamanders and a collection of insects take refuge and feed from them. A tree contributes as much to the fabric of the living in death as in life.

For some people, the same is true.

Mary has died. Her son comes to knock at the door of the Blue House, where he grew up. Amid the music and the smell of cooking, amid the chaos and the strident cries of the living, his eyes roam the walls, brush over what remains of his past and the courageous mother who has just left us.

He doesn't want to come in; he remains frozen between two steps, trapped in the brutal, beautiful chasm, raw. Mary died in her old folks' home, surrounded by astronaut orderlies, empathetic behind their visors.

Mary, who delighted in what abounded and throbbed. Mary, the savourer, do you remember the little bright blue flowers that sprung up around your pretty house? I asked you what they were called. The bright blue of your eyes gave the answer before your voice. 'Forget-me-nots. That's their name, Anaïs. Forget-me-nots.'

I will not forget you.

Your forget-me-nots still grow all around.

And the long months spent here have allowed us to rediscover around us the flowers that you sowed but that the rest of our lives used to swallow up.

Your hand drew a floral moat, which forever rings the house, and we are slowly learning its music.

The children sprinkle their meals with petals of your bergamot, chase garter snakes under your quince tree, and seek shade under your lupins.

Your son has to leave. He will return with your dust, which he will put where it wants to go on this land that already knows you.

I want to see my near-grandmother, Janine. I don't want her to die like Mary, alone in Montréal, in her long-term-care facility. But I am not allowed to visit; only one person is. My mother tells me about their tête-à-têtes. Her head is hidden behind a visor. Just like a goalie. She finds Janine in clothes that are too big, her pants undone. She dresses her properly. Puts on a clean shirt, does her hair, draws her fine grey hair behind her ears.

Janine has pictures of us in her room, but she doesn't know who we are. She isn't sad. She has her battery-powered cat; she likes it and thinks it's alive. She still calls it Albert, after the first and last man of her life.

My mother takes out Scrabble. The goalie plays the woman in the flowered shirt.

Janine plays the word *whiskey*. One hundred and forty-four points in one go.

My mother smiles behind her mask. One–nothing.

Janine tells her that 'it's nice here. The décor is pretty,' but she will have to go soon. Her sister will be expecting her.

She thinks she is a guest. My mother is reassured that she thinks the long-term-care facility is nice. Asks her if at home, where Pauline is waiting, it's nice too.

'Yes, it's nice too,' Janine answers.

Perfect. A gift for happiness.

Janine's rust-brown eyes search my mother's face.

'And who are you?'

My mother answers: 'I'm your daughter.' Janine is happy about this good news.

'Really?'

My mother points to a picture of her hanging on the wall. Janine exclaims, 'Aren't you pretty!' before asking gently, 'And what is your name?'

My mother, just as gently, asks her what she thinks her name is. Janine hesitates, searches, and finds it.

'I think your name is Robert.'

Behind her visor, my mother laughs. Two–nothing.

Janine doesn't know exactly who my mother is, but she knows that she loves her and my mother loves her back. Two–all.

When I was little, Janine's brother, my grandfather Marcel, made me a dollhouse, with two storeys and many rooms. We get it out of the basement. It smells like earth, and its walls are peeling. It still has its little cotton curtains in the windows, carefully hung with his fingertips.

I imagine him threading them on tiny rods and mounting them on the walls of my house.

My grandfather Marcel was a painter. He studied at the École du Meuble, a furniture-making school, where his teacher was Paul-Émile Borduas. His project for his master's degree was building a family home, with two children's bedrooms and a large dining room. He designed it. But never built it. His wife left, and he did too.

My dollhouse is the house he dreamed of before the big departures, before the scars.

In the basement, we find some old wallpaper that belonged to Mary. Little blue and red flowers commingle on the paper, which we cut up and use to cover the walls of the miniature house. We also get out the dregs of a can of paint the colour of the Blue House and happily smear the bare walls.

We place Marcel's house, which is joyous again, under the apple tree, in front of the river. Deer come to eat alongside it, and snails have chosen it as their domicile.

'Snails making love!'

A long and fascinating spectacle. The children take their places, discreet in their yellow slickers.

The embrace of the snails must be taking this long because the animals are in deep negotiation. Both are almost fully out of their shell, infinitely vulnerable, and they are hesitating about which part of themselves to offer the other. Because snails are both male and female. The lovers can therefore reveal themselves as male and offer sperm or as female and release eggs.

It all depends on who the embrace is shared with, hence the length of the discussion, necessary to the actual encounter.

In a given individual, the male is revealed more easily than the female, who protects herself and presents herself to the other only when she feels safe. If there are several other possible conquests around the snail, the male will probably emerge, the female being reserved for the meeting with the best match.

The wallpaper starts to ripple. It is raining on the lovers, who end up choosing the bathroom in Marcel's house, with a herd of children watching, rooting them on.

My grandfather Marcel was always parsimonious with tender words. Maybe he was protecting himself. Maybe those words create permanent openings, windows to sensitivity, which would be difficult to close. When death drew nearer, he joined us in the valley. He was thin; he had practically stopped eating, had difficulty talking. But he wanted to be surrounded by his children and his grandchildren.

We celebrated. With him in the middle, near death. And with children, and babies, and oysters because he liked them.

He said 'I love you' to my mother. It was the first time.

He could no longer stand unassisted, but he could still hold his brush, like a life preserver, and, in the morning, he would wake up at five to paint.

Feisty and impertinent, he sent his colours to the canvas as if he were seventeen years old.

A few minutes before his last breath, my mother slipped his long brush, his companion, between his thin fingers. He brought it to his heart and quietly died.

I have his final painting in my house. Yellow and youthful. Strident.

We are popping into the city.

My eldest is holding his precious package on his lap: his promises of skipping.

We return in silence to the deserted city, with the feeling of having abandoned it, wondering whether we will still be able to love it.

Long, patient lines stretch in front of the stores.

Mouths hidden behind masks mean that eyes suddenly capture all the attention: two breaches to the inside, becoming the only tellers of resistance, fear, and doubt, the only conveyers of hugs and handshakes.

Two pretty mirrors, two little commas that wait for what's next and that carry the voice of the whole body.

The streets are otherwise empty.

Montréal is iced over, on alert, frozen in an unknown time. My city is traumatized. Immobilized before two headlights coming on too fast, illuminating nothing good. My city is frightened, and so am I.

Tall and thin, his blond hair cascading in waves down his back, he has been standing in the window forever, waiting for her to arrive.

There she is. Loup bounds toward his teacher, his box in his hands.

They're standing two metres from each other, and he can't contain his joy, which colonizes the empty space, erases the distance and renders it obsolete. Loup's joy takes the world by storm, and suddenly the whole street is more alive: nothing can resist the radiance of childhood.

Loup proudly gives his teacher the gift. She will have to find a river or a lake.

It's a refreshing mission, and she is happy.

He tells her about his fruitful, adventurous picking of fiddleheads, manages to tell her he misses her and his friends, that he misses learning.

He has read all the *Harry Potters*, some of them two or three times. Now he is discovering the memoirs of Pierre-Esprit Radisson and leading an army of ninjas from the valley.

He is learning to walk on the edge of his precipices; he knows them without understanding them. He is trying to tame the emptiness, not to flee it, to see what is just beyond.

He would like to get back to class and to the teacher who makes nets to catch him when he falls. But that is impossible, and he holds back tears because, after all, he is growing up. She smiles at him: she has confidence in him.

Camille heads back along the pavement, her skipping stones in her pockets.

Loup watches her go so he doesn't fall, little tightrope walker balancing between two ages.

I put three more pieces of toast in front of heads still heavy from the night, eyes that have not lifted the veil that protects them from the day. I go back to the counter to make some more and to watch them from behind: their little tender necks and their tangled hair.

First they eat in silence, then their voices emerge in unison in a joyful staccato. They rise with the sun over the city.

Now they are bubbling and ready to devour the day.

In the doorway, I adjust the hem of a pant, I wipe the corner of a mouth, and I redo a braid.

I reappropriate the meaning of these gestures.

I'm the one who decides on the grandeur of the ordinary.

The door slams on my foot, which I leave there, between indoors and out.

The children rush to the park, the eldest leading the race: charge!

My daughter looks back at me. I can't see her lips, but I hear her shout over the mask, over everything: 'Maman! You can't tell, but underneath, I'M SMILING!'

The joy has been transmitted, and it will survive me.

My children get further away, become smaller, and yet they grow bigger.

I close the door on the interiors that have grown nobler. The most beautiful miracles are ordinary.

Some biologists refer to trees as individuals. An individual sycamore or an individual willow. It is an improper use of the term, botanist Francis Hallé explains.

We can definitely refer to individual animals, because, like human animals, they are indivisible.

We cannot separate a human or a cat into several parts: it would die.

But a tree is divisible. A single tree can exist in several other trees. That is what makes it a hundred years old, a thousand years old, and, in some cases, immortal. When it is worn out and too old, an extension of it takes the baton, and the tree is perpetuated by an extension of the extension, and so on.

The tree is a divisible living being. It is one, together.

My family history is woven from abandonment. On both sides of the ocean, the tie was severed, people left and didn't come back, leaving a bunch of little holes in those who came after.

So I endlessly knit myself ties. I light fires so the night will never come.

I build myself a constellation of magnets that keep me grounded.

I meet the woodsman in a brown motel on the corner of a busy street. I duck in quickly, looking down at the orange carpet, which holds the memory of the dirty, hurried steps of bodies seeking each other.

The room is small, the window opening onto an impenetrable brick wall.

Naked in a lost town.

The man evaporates without the forest. He doesn't quench me anymore.

I head out alone into the night. Over my shoulder, Mont Royal asks me a question.

I climb it slowly. I take my time. I have walked it hundreds of times, but this time is new.

I meet its red maples, sugar maples, white birches, ashes, red oaks, ironwoods, hawthorns, black cherries, shagbark hickories, green ashes, cedars, elms, and I arrive at the top as if coming home.

My city is awake and twinkling despite the pain.

*T*YTIRUS: *Yes, Love together with the Tree can in our minds unite into one sole idea. The one and the other are something which, born of an imperceptible germ, grows ever larger and ever stronger, spreads and branches forth; but so far as it rises towards heaven (or happiness) just so much must it down descend into the dark substance of that which we unknowingly are.*

LUCRETIUS: *Our earth? ...*

TYTIRUS: *Yes ... And it is there, in the depths of the shades wherein melt and are mingled what there is of our human kind, and what there is of our living substance, and what there is of our memories and of our hidden strengths and weaknesses ... that there is to be found what I called the 'spring of tears.'*

LUCRETIUS: *You go far for a shepherd. Do you then always weep?*

– Paul Valéry
'Dialogue of the Tree'

I come home tense and fragmented from a day in the city. It had been a while. My days were modelled on roundness and this one, in a grid, speaks to me of my life before.

My taxi driver, svelte with grey hair, an elegant Haitian man, does not say a word the whole trip. He slows down as he passes the two 'sleeping police' in front of my house. That's what speed bumps are called in creole: sleeping police. There are two across from the little park in front of my Yellow House.

While I dig for my money, I see his shoulders drop, his body relax and come down a few floors. A sigh fogs the plexiglass that separates us.

'Is everything okay, Monsieur?'

He turns to collect the fare.

He apologizes immediately and drops his tear-filled eyes.

I can make out the slow smile that, behind the mask, gradually spreads across his handsome face.

'The children … '

I understand that he is talking about the children playing in the park. The daycare across the way has let its hordes of children out to frolic. Little humans, two or three years old, scream and shout and laugh and cry while they advance like little hammers driving in the nail of their arrival in the world. They are here. Their imperfect song spreads before us like a carpet of promise.

The old man places his hands on the steering wheel, worn from all the trips, worn from having become the only thing to hang on to so as not to fall.

'It helps.'

'Yes, it helps.'

I get out, and he stays there for a moment, taking in this concentrated pulse of vitality like a lifesaving fix.

In the park, people are settled everywhere, and I look at them as if for the first time. They are new. They take their space in these dark, shaky times.

A man and a woman, at either end of a bench, share two long fits of unbridled laughter that merge together, melt into each other.

A family has laid a tablecloth like a buoy on the grass and is picnicking. A baby buddha is tasting something for the first time, and the parents get excited watching him taste something for the first time.

A girl. A girl dancing. A girl dancing alone. Her headset in her ears, her clothes hugging her curves, her waves; her generous body carves out space with strokes of sensuality. She closes her eyes, giving herself over to this happy resistance. She grooves big against the end of the world. She doesn't care about what is dying.

At her feet, a miracle. Bouquets of sweet white clover break through the concrete.

We are adrift.

If we lash ourselves to what is growing, we will not fall any farther.

Courage is a measure of our heartfelt participation with life, with another, [...] with a future. To be courageous is not necessarily to go anywhere or to do anything except to make conscious those things we already feel deeply and then to live through the unending vulnerabilities of those consequences.

– David Whyte, poet

It's my turn to teach class. The children are waiting for me outdoors.

'Mamaaaaaan!'
   'Coming!'

Crouched around the chicken coop, the five children are still in pyjamas.

Today's lesson: demystifying chickens.

They know we are talking about them; they circle us, curious.

Are they intelligent?

Some yesses burst forth, some nos too. My five students, extremely interested, disagree.

According to what I have read, chickens can recognize around eighty of their friends. They can tell them apart.

A quintet of *wows*. Heartfelt and impressed.

Chickens have an intelligence quotient of between 100 and 125. The equivalent of a seven-year-old child.

Noé is as intelligent as a chicken!

The three children who are under seven remain silent.

Attentive, suspicious looks toward the birds, who are pecking around us: respect.

Now, why eggs?

A chicken releases an ovule every day. It goes on a long journey inside the animal, during which is formed the yolk, the white, then the shell. If there is a rooster, the ovule may be fertilized and produce an egg filled with a chick. Otherwise, it's an egg we can eat.

The children jump around a little. Runny noses and itchy bums. Plus the ball that has deflated, which will have to be seen to.

Just a minute: class isn't over.

The anatomy of the chicken: under its beak, the wattle; behind its comb, the lobe.

They tune out; I've lost them.

Okay. Let's move on to practical exercises. Let's clean out the chicken coop.

The perch is dirty; the rest is pretty clean. That is where our chickens spend most of their nights; during the day they live outside.

'And why do they sleep only up high, on their perch?

'Because chickens used to be wild birds and were domesticated by humans. At night, they perched up high, on the branches of a tree, so they could avoid the many predators on the ground. Since they can't fly to get away, the trees became their refuge.'

'But chickens in trees was a long time ago.'

I check my notes.

'Yes, it was six thousand years ago.'

'So our chickens, they sleep up high because they remember the danger and the trees that protect them?'

' … Yes, an ancient memory tells them about going up high. An instinct that was passed on through thousands of years.'

An admiring silence settles in. Even the chickens seem proud.

My daughter asks me if she has one too, an ancient memory.

'I don't know … I would imagine.'

'So, you too, Maman?'

'Yes. Me too.'

Somewhere, I have an ancient memory.

From the other side of the road, between the garden and the house, the large oak whispers. Under the tree, in the earth, lie the seeds of future oaks. Some acorns have fallen from its own branches and buried themselves in the ground; others were carried by the wind, the birds, or the squirrels. Some come from this oak, others do not.

The roots of the oak stretch out underground. They are powerful and territorial. They brutalize and crush nascent seeds, preventing them from growing in the shade of the master oak.

But not all. Because the oak has a sense of family. The tree recognizes the seeds that come from its branches, and its roots grow around them, with difficulty, but with great care. The oak protects its children and destroys those of the others.

My mother has always gathered cushions of moss from the forest. Her wicker basket on her arm, she walks softly and carefully detaches the cap from the rocks. She makes them living islands that she sets in her house, where she can lose herself when she needs to. Because my mother can shrink when she wants and go for a walk inside. Sometimes she does it when things get too serious. I think it's a pretty safe way to escape.

A nineteenth-century entomologist named Humboldt decided one day to describe, in a single book, all that is *at present known of celestial and terrestrial phenomena, from the nature of the nebula down to the geography of the mosses clinging to a granite rock.*

Moss is five hundred million years old. It survives the winter by crystallizing, emptied of its water, and retakes its shape during the first thaw, gorging itself on the moisture generated.

It is the filigree that enables the soil to remain soil, generously absorbing the spring rain.

It is a micro-forest, structured and alive.

Without roots, it nourishes itself from the air, storing its acid and toxic metals. So it cleans the rain. It does this so well that at the end of the stream, in New York City, the decision was made to protect a mountain and its moss rather than building a water treatment plant.

So much power sitting in the hands of my mother, who collects things that repair.

The fog masks the mountain and the stream flows. Like yesterday. The children emerge from sleep. A distracted eye on the outdoors. The chicken coop grate has fallen.

'Did you go get the eggs this morning?'

This gesture has been a prelude to every morning: bare little feet in the wet grass running to get breakfast just laid. Eggs still warm, compared for size. The lighthearted pride of being in cahoots with the animals.

'No.'

I tear down the steps, push open the door and advance, my stomach in a knot, to what I can already make out is a tragedy.

Not the mountain, or the fog, or the stream can cushion the moment I see her. Feathers first. Whole wings torn off. A chicken still standing, immobile and quiet, the face ripped off. An eye is missing, there is blood everywhere, the remains of a beak dangling.

The others have been gutted, entrails spilled, bloody, already covered in flies.

It smells like iron. Warm blood, meat.

I scream.

The children are at the window.

'Stay away.'

Their father isn't here, and neither are his large arms or his courage.

The others are gone too, lucky for them: a few days to breathe, a few days to remember who they are.

Barefoot on the dirt road, I call my parents.

My body is trembling.

The faceless chicken looks at me with the half of an eye that remains. Standing in the middle of the others, feet in the blood, she lays an egg. A warm egg, which passes through her plucked, wounded body. I am angry with her for making this cruel offering.

The chicken is struggling to breathe, a weak rattle passes through her, a wisp of air that still finds its way. My mother reads that you have to cover her wounds with green clay. I have some.

My father holds the surviving chicken in his hands while I apply layers of viscous mud, heavy and sticky, to her wounds. She closes her eye. It's as if she is holding back from dying.

I place her in a box in the house, on a little bed of straw, safe from the flies.

We shovel the chicken entrails. The smell of their death makes its way into my mouth, builds up in my saliva.

I try to distract us, to invent something that can hold us above the tragedy.

I preserve chanterelles with my eldest. I tear his guilt from him. It's my fault he didn't close the fence to the chicken coop. It stays stuck in my throat, but he is breathing easier.

Picking herbs in the garden, thinly slicing the garlic, boiling it all for three minutes in cider vinegar, covering it with olive oil.

In the next room, the chicken whistles and gasps for air.

I won't survive its presence in the house.

I have seen dead bodies in Nablus, Soweto, Sao Paulo.

But I will not survive a disfigured chicken gasping for air in my living room.

I have to kill it.

I tell the children.

The two little ones cry and protest. The eldest hides out in a book.

I dig a hole.

My father arrives with his axe.

He will do it for me. He has seen his grandfather do it before.

It is a gesture of immense love.

My father is such a gentle man.

I join the children to make a bouquet.

They are the only ones who can tell the chickens apart.

A bouquet of red bergamot for Gourmandise trembles in their hands, and my father calls out to us.

It's done.

New blood on the ground.

Little feet walk in it and head to the hole.

We had already covered up the others. But Gourmandise's orange feathers are still shining in the sun, looking beautiful and alive.

My youngest screams. We set down the flowers. We cover the bird with earth, then rocks.

Thanks for the eggs.

I hug my father. His grandfather skinned rabbits on the other side of the ocean: it's a long way to reach back, in memory, on land, in the body.

My father cut off the head of my disfigured chicken out of love.

She ran around with no head before collapsing for good.

In another life, we would have eaten her. But I am a tourist in this rural world.

Too sensitive and entirely breakable.

My parents have left.

I am alone in pieces with my children, huddled against their shocked bodies.

We watch three Walt Disneys in a row, wrapped in each other's arms.

Like a whole. Death with us.

Still hung from the windows, our sweet clover has dried. In the bathroom, its fragrance mixes with a child's poo that's floating in the toilet.

The flowers drop off, fall to the ground in the dust. I wearily pull down the dried bouquets. I want to throw them out. I could throw them out. I am tired.

I am beached on the living room floor.

I want to keep the idea going for my son. Seeing me carefully strip the stems, he joins me. And then so do all the children. Their little fingers pull the flowers from the branches, grip them like little buoys. We don't speak. We receive communion. Saved, for a moment.

The same little fingers will soon dust cakes with sweet clover flowers.

And when they taste it, all the months gone by will seep into their mouths.

Hermann, more stooped and thinner, but just as proud, is bent over his documents.

On the window ledge, the sun spills onto an old photo of Angélique in his arms. They are young and in love.

Firm and straight, he slides a drawing toward me. It is his land, his trees that stretch to the side of the mountain, his string of ponds, his moss roads and their little bridges carefully drawn above the waters they cross.

His vast kingdom is at the border of my parents' kingdom. Hermann will die, and he fears there will be a gash on his land. Angélique does not want this place without him. She will go be with her children in the big city; she will go moor her heart somewhere else.

Hermann asks whether I want to take care of his trails. Whether I want to walk in his footsteps. Whether I want to embrace the fragile immensity of his land and protect it.

I do.

His long fingers slowly follow the trails on paper, drawn with lead pencil on his homemade maps.

He stops at the first bridge, then at the second. It is almost as if he is going for a dip. His fingers progress toward the majestic curve of the pasture, caressing the contour before plunging back into the little woods. I place my hand on his, right there, at the beginning of the forest.

On paper, in an almost straight line, the tops of the trees whirl in a row of childlike clouds drawn in pencil.

On land, it is the place where the long field ends, where the trees begin. It is where the sky hides, swallowed by the birches, the beeches, and the maples. It is where the covered ground smells of humus and moss. Where you can hear the song of frogs at night. It is the edge of the pond, the refuge of the bittern, the start of the empire of the Canada goose.

I tell him this is where my love and I kissed for the first time. We were sleeping in the field, behind the Red House. A festive campground like every summer. That one was the last. Maybe, from the start, he was the one I was searching for, tent to tent.

That afternoon, coming back from a dip, we cut through the woods behind Hermann's house. I introduced him to the chickadees, the sparrows, and the turtledoves that still live there. We plucked from the ground flowers and pieces of clothing dropped by friends who had gone on ahead of us. A sock, a bathing suit, a hat, a pack of cigarettes: traces of an adolescent Hansel.

The forest protected us and, just before I left his arms, just before the sun and the eyes of others were on us, we kissed. I think I was the one who chose it.

Hermann knows that I will learn to read his land like the largest, most sensitive, and most important of stories.

Our fingers continue their slow journey along the small map. The beeches blowing in the wind seem to bow as we pass.

We advance in step on the same drawing, and when Hermann stops at the base of a tree, I wait for him in silence. But he doesn't come. He has stopped moving.

I turn toward him. He is gone.

In his place stands a bittern, tracing a long S on the edge of the ponds. A sudden breeze hits it, and its neck stretches toward the sky, its beak makes a bridge between two stretches of blue and its entire body blends into the marshland.

The bird then undulates slowly to the rhythm of what surrounds it. It is visible only to the eyes of the plants. Hermann becomes one with the land that brought him into this world.

Wendy's tractor rumbles at the end of the road.

I station myself at the side of the road, and I wait. Wendy slows as she approaches; I signal to her to stop. She cuts the engine, and we look at each other for a moment in an intimidating silence.

She tells me, in the singsong accent she picked up from her father, that there is so much work, that she is trying to take over where Clark Kent left off, 'but he was everywhere, so … '

She sees me look at her in the tractor. She knows the effort of substitution that demands; succession is brutal. I think she is pretty. She sees that too.

Her moon face reveals a smile that eclipses the sun.

She has to go. She has a story to continue.

I try my luck. I ask her where her father got the stones to shore up the foundations of our homes.

She stares at me now, caught in the net of filial secrecy. 'I don't know.'

So I ask her in another way. 'I know your father carefully chose each of the stones that hold up the houses in the area. But mine has found other footholds, and I have an orphan tombstone on my conscience.'

I climb the hill to the children's hideout.

They are in the middle of World War II. The Axis forces are invading, and the Allies are catapulting acorns in a vicious counterattack.

With the back of my hand, I push away the wooden weapons that shroud Jeanne d'Arc, and I take her in my arms.

The children protest: I just tore away the door of the prison.

'Where are you going with that?'

'I'm bringing her back where she belongs.'

A small square of forest was cleared to let graves grow. They put the Catholics on one side and the Protestants on the other. A divided territory, even in death.

The children are running around, overexcited to be so close to the dead.

We are looking for a grave in the middle of the cemetery.

The hundred gravestones pierce the soil like worn flags. They sum up a life as well as they can, in a few engraved letters.

Our strong, insolent bodies walk on death in the sun, walk on death in the colour and the end of summer.

Dandelion fluff floats to me. I blow hard on it, and Jacquot shows me the way: at the back of the cemetery, a gravestone is leaning to the right, unsteady. It seems pensive.

Purple lichen has filled the depression of its letters: *Royal Lamoureux, husband of Jeanne d'Arc.*

Flowers have grown in the empty space the stone leans toward. Bellflowers, veronicas, forget-me-nots, adorned with a carpet of tall ferns. Ferns whose fronds are a head taller than the children.

Everything is beyond us here.

The plants have covered the cavity left by Jeanne d'Arc, transforming it into full, vibrant absence.

All around us, the cemetery seems punctuated with colourful gaps. Dozens of secret graves, the stones of which are buried somewhere nearby, solid mortars for other lives.

I lean Jeanne d'Arc's gravestone against Royal's. Now she is resting precariously between the ground and her love.

'Let's go.'

The children scream, as if something in them has just understood that the end is not so far away. They scream too loud, they laugh too hard, they become complete, visceral exclamations, disoriented by death.

I take a few steps; Jeanne d'Arc's stone leaves Royal's shoulder, pitches and slides to the ground. I break my momentum to replace it.

A wisp of air between the two, a view of the birds and a bed of ferns.

I leave her finally exactly there.

'Let's go!'

The children follow me this time. Suddenly solemn, precisely connected to the ephemeral. They salute their ally as they pass.

'Goodbye, Jeanne d'Arc. See you later.'

Behind the vegetable garden, the memory of the mass grave has been dug up by the animals. No truce possible: the wilderness wins. The bodies of our chickens are again scattered on the ground, their red feathers flying in the wind, an echo of our pain.

There it is. I see its impertinent ardour on display.

I advance on tiptoe through everything that has grown, everything I have sown.

Squash, mainly.

A smooth chili gleams at the end of its stem, proud and strident.

I pick the chili, stuff it in my mouth. I crunch the fruit, which explodes and fills me to the back of my throat, burns my tongue, my palate, storms my stomach.

It is not the flesh or the seeds that sting. It is the pith, inside the pepper, on which the seeds grow. The pith of the bird's eye chili sets my mouth on fire.

'Why are you crying, Maman?'
    'I'm not, it's the chili.'

I go back into this house where the sun, a regular, drifts in.

The love of my life is sitting at the piano with his back to me.

The keyboard is worn; there are notes missing; the music comes out of it in a clump, dusty and inelegant. The mice have made a nest between the strings.

My man's back takes up five octaves. His broad, gentle shoulders have carried our three children from one end of the country to the other.

He doesn't let his fingers roam over the keyboard. He plunges them into it. He sets to the keys, grabs on to them.

This man is sailing through his turmoil, and I am the witness to his rescues.

He is a miracle every second, and in this one precisely, I never want to lose him again. I make a place for myself between him and the piano. I kiss him. It's hot and it burns.

My searing saliva mixes with his.

I love him, and I want to choose him until my death.

The walls of the Blue House suddenly creak. The day rolls over us. In the rays of light the branches of the black maple stretch out, penetrating the house, brushing our skin.

The wind harnesses the space, the ceilings crack and crumble around us, grass grows under our feet, dew beads on our eyelashes.

We merge with each other, and our three children hang on to our intertwined bodies, like three shells on a rock. A warm, heavy moss climbs our legs, invades the folds of our skin, wraps around us.

The forest runs in our blood. Our five hearts beat in time with the earth and mix with the rain, which is now falling on us.

There are no more doors or walls, no more contours or boundaries.

There is just outdoors, which entwines with our bodies.

We are together, woven with the remains of the living.

Fragile. Rooted. Miraculous survivors.

ACKNOWLEDGEMENTS

Thank you to the residents of the valley.

Thank you to La Maison d'Ariane and the Jardins de Métis, Claudine Roy, Catherine Gagnon, Ludovic Jolicoeur, and the St. Lawrence River for the writing nooks.

Thank you to Francis Hallé and Romain Bertrand for the lines of thought and intelligence about what is sensitive.

Thank you to Mélanie Vincelette for the faith and courage.

Thank you to all those I have loved and all those I love. You are my country.